Ellen wanted that ten-speed bicycle
in Niemeyer's window more than
anything in the world.
Why else would she have agreed to
spend a whole summer of her
life "lady-sitting" for
seventy-seven-year-old Lilith Adams?
How could she have known in June
how much she would come to
enjoy the days with Lilith, and how
much she would grow to love
and respect Lilith's strength,
wisdom, and independence?

Through weeks filled with shared
experiences and adventures,
twelve-year-old Ellen overcomes her
initial resistance and grows to
understand the feelings and
the special concerns of older people.
She learns how they face loneliness,
alcoholism, insecurity, and—
most important—the need to give
and to receive love.

The summer becomes the unforgettable
Lilith Summer. A book for all
ages—for grandmothers to give to
granddaughters, and granddaughters to
give to grandmothers.

THE Lilith Summer

BY HADLEY IRWIN

THE FEMINIST PRESS

Old Westbury, New York

Published in the United States by The Feminist Press,
Box 334, Old Westbury, New York 11568.

First edition, third printing

LIBRARY OF CONGRESS CATALOGING IN PUBLICATION DATA:

Irwin, Hadley.
The Lilith Summer.
    Summary: A 12-year-old girl relates her experiences
during the summer she spends as a companion to
a 77-year-old woman.
    [1. Old age—Fiction] I. Title.
PZ7.I712Li   [Fic]   78-24379   ISBN 0-912670-51-7

With special acknowledgment to Ellen and Bill Dorsch
for their kind assistance.

Cover and Interior Design by Susan Trowbridge
Cover Illustration by Sandra Wakeen

ACKNOWLEDGMENTS

Special thanks are due to Maia Wojciechowska for her suggestions and encouragement when *The Lilith Summer* was in the planning stage and to Sharon Wigutoff and Jeanne Bracken for their perceptive editorial advice.

HADLEY IRWIN

CONTENTS

THE Lilith Summer

To Ann
and to Lee,
of course

THE BEGINNING

I FINALLY AGREED, and only because I wanted the ten-speed Raleigh in Neimeyer's window, to spend the days of that summer—just the days, not the nights—as a paid companion to Lilith Adams.

"She needs someone. And Eunice will pay you. Fifteen dollars a week. That's a hundred and fifty dollars for the summer. If you really want that bicycle. . . ."

The ten-speed had a chrome-plated steel frame with a bright blue racing saddle, dual extension brake levers with blue wrapped handles, black rat-trap pedals, handlebar gearshift, and rear disc brakes.

1

IT TOOK BOTH MY HANDS to tug open the gate.

The iron weight, chained to the corner post, flung the steel tubing back against my ankle as I slipped through. I crouched on the walk between the borders of iris and rubbed the spot of pain.

White curtains hung motionless against the bay window. The door, full-paned, was carefully draped against peering in, but thinly veiled for peeking out. But no one was peeking out, even though the clang of the front gate should have alerted the neighborhood that Lilith Adams was having company that morning.

The walk circled the corner of the white frame house. I wondered if I should use the back door.

A companion for seventy-seven-year-old Lilith Adams. All summer. The back door would be best.

Two crossed blue eyes glowered at me from the top of the clothesline post. Black ears, black nose, black-tipped tail, and black paws on the buckskin body of a huge Siamese. I saw the body tense.

I wasn't afraid of cats, but this. . . . I had read how Siamese cats were once trained to perch above castle doors and pounce on thieves trying to carry off the king's jewels.

I edged nearer the house, the Siamese eyes following me, measuring, calculating. My back brushed the iron railing of the steps. The cat rose to full height, balancing. I could not retreat.

"Here, kitty . . . kitty. . . ."

The animal flexed its legs, arched its back, eyes never shifting. I put one foot on the first step. It flicked its tail and opened its mouth, red and enormous, in a fearful "Meeeowl."

Where was Lilith Adams? She knew I was coming.

"Mrs. Adams!" I bolted up the steps and wrenched open the screen door.

"What is it?" came a voice from the darkened room.

The kitchen smelled of coffee and cinnamon toast. A woman stood in the doorway.

"My cat?"

She moved toward me, bringing the scent of Ivory soap and cloves.

"I like cats . . . and I'm not really scared . . . but. . . ."

"He's all show, that Lord Jim."

"Lord Jim?"

"You'll see through him when you get acquainted. But sometimes introductions are necessary. Come along."

She seized my hand and led me out through the screen door.

"Lord Jim!" Her voice was the voice of God. "What's the matter with you? This is Ellen. Ellen will be here . . . with us . . . the rest of the summer."

The Siamese lunged from his perch, landing at the woman's feet, and rubbed his back against her legs.

"Pet him." It was a command. "He understands now."

I touched Lord Jim's neck, and as he stretched sideways, I slipped my fingers into the tiny indentations behind his ears.

"He's telling you to scratch him. He likes that."

His eyes softened as I moved my fingers around his ears and down his back. He flattened himself upon the sidewalk and purred.

"You scared me, Lord Jim."

"He was just putting on his Frankenstein act. Lord Jim's a terrible ham."

I turned to look up at the woman, ashamed of my fear. Her face was old, wrinkled at the corners of the eyes and at the edges of the mouth, cheeks and flesh under the chin sagging. Her hair was white—white like milkweed silk; the eyes, milky blue.

The woman stared down as if seeing beyond me—far, far beyond me and the morning and the June day.

"Lord Jim won't frighten you again." Another command.

"Now, Lord Jim. Get up and be about your own business. Ellen and I have things to do."

We sat in the kitchen, Lilith Adams at one end of the old table and I at the other, and I began to wonder if a ten-speed Raleigh bicycle could be worth a ten-week Lilith summer.

"I trust we can get along for ten weeks."

Her words were as formal as a long-distance call.

She clasped her hands before her on the table. The skin was yellow and dry and wrinkled like the skin of an onion, veins pushing between knuckles up into crooked fingers. She saw me looking. Her jaw muscle tightened. She straightened in her chair and thrust her hands into her lap.

I looked at the floor, up the wall to the ceiling, and back down again to the floor.

"Yeah. I hope so too."

What did you say to old people? They moved so slowly and left gaping holes in their talk. And their eyes—cloudy.

"I tell you. . . ."

Her voice was as fierce as if we'd been quarreling.

"What?"

She did not answer. It was like trying to talk to someone on a ferris wheel. You waited for them to come down to make them hear you.

"I said 'What?' "

"What what?"

"You said, 'I tell you' and I said, 'What?' Now I'm asking you, 'What did you tell me?' "

"I said I hope we can get along for ten weeks."

"I hope so too. But you said that once."

"I did?"

THAT FIRST MORNING I dusted her stuff in the living room.

"Not on the tops. I can do that. Around the bottoms. I can't stoop very well."

I ran down to the grocery store.

"Pick up a loaf of day-old bread. It's in the cart by the check-out counter."

I swept off the front walk.

"That walk gets longer every day."

And I carried a dishpan full of fruit jars down into the cellar.

"Eunice said I wasn't to try that again. That's what put me in the nursing home for three months, a tumble down those steps."

After lunch she took a nap.

"Why don't you go out and play?"

"Out and play!" Who did she think I was? I was twelve.

I finally escaped to a grassy spot under the branches of a weeping willow in the backyard. I wanted to cry, but no matter how tightly I squeezed my eyes shut, tears would not come. Everything was so old—the tree, the house, Lilith Adams.

Why did Lilith's daughter offer money? Why did my mother offer *me*? Why did my mother go off to summer school? And why did Lilith have to be so old?

Maybe I would quit. But how else could I earn enough in one summer to buy a ten-speed? I could pretend to come to Lilith's and then not show up. But Mother would find out.

Maybe Lilith would die. Some morning when I opened the back screen door and looked in the kitchen, Lilith would be lying on the floor, all purple and dead. I'd have to call the police or the fire department or the ambulance or something. I'd look up those phone numbers and write them down, just in case.

"Ellen."

I did not move. A lady bug scuttled along a branch in front of my nose and onto a leaf, skirting the outer edges.

"Ellen!"

The voice was sharper.

Maybe it was time to go home. I crawled out from under the willow.

"Oh, there you are. I'm going to have my tea now. You have some too."

She didn't look at me. She gazed past me and up to the topmost branch of the willow.

"There are cookies on the kitchen counter."

They were homemade peanut butter cookies with criss-crossed fork marks on top like tic-tac-toes.

We sat again at the big table, Lilith at one end and I at the other, and I tasted hot ginger tea for the first time.

The big hand on the wind-up clock on Lilith's kitchen shelf took a full sixty minutes to inch the little hand from four to five. Finally, it finished its circle.

"Can I go home now?"

"Is it five?"

"It's five."

"You can go home."

FORTY-NINE DAYS TO GO

I RAN—THAT FIRST DAY—all the way uphill to Farley's cotton-wood and didn't slow down until I was nearly home. I breathed through my mouth, trying to get rid of the taste of Lilith's house. It tasted old. It tasted musty. Musty on towels and rugs, on blankets and walls, in bedrooms, in closets, like a mouthful of lake water.

I ran—still seeing the picture in Lilith's bedroom of a wolf on a snowy hill, mouth open, head tipped back with icicles hanging from his jowls, howling at the moon.

I ran—trying to forget the house of Lilith and the clock with the two-pound can of pepper as big as a brick beside it.

"Why so much pepper?"

"Oh, it came in such a lovely can."

And no place to go, the house a circle from kitchen to dining room to living room to front bedroom to spare bedroom to kitchen.

I ran because I knew I was caught in the circle of that house for the rest of the summer.

SKEET BARCLAY WAS MOWING our lawn as I dashed up the walk.

"Getting home from the baby-sitter's?"

I tried to ignore him. Skeet was the biggest klutz in our school. Well, almost. Maybe Tarp Wilson was, but Skeet was a close second.

"Didn't ya hear me? I asked if you was just getting back from your baby-sitter's."

I picked up a handful of grass and threw it at him. He ducked. I gathered another handful.

"Did you take your nap today, baby? Did she read you some little stories?"

I hit him that time, right in the face.

"She's not my baby-sitter, you jerk. I sit with *her*. 'Cause she's so old she can't stay alone," I screamed as I headed for the house. "And I bet I make a lot more money than you do mowing lawns."

A wet glob of grass cuttings caught me in the back of the head and skittered across the front step as I burst through the door.

"Honestly, Ellen. Must you be so noisy?" Mother was home. Her books were piled on the dining room table. "I can hear you from the minute you leave Lilith's."

"Skeet was chasing me. What's for supper?"

I headed for the kitchen.

"It's on the stove. We'll be eating late tonight."

I got the last can of Pepsi from the refrigerator, climbed up on the bar stool, and leaned my head in my hands.

"How was the first day?" Mother sat down beside me, a pencil tucked behind her ear, her eyes scanning a notebook.

"Rotten!"

"Oh?"

Mother was not listening.

"I said *rotten*. Do I have to go back tomorrow?"

She was listening now.

"Why of course you have to go back tomorrow."

"But, Mom. It's so awful. Boring. Long. She's . . . she's so *old*. She keeps saying things and forgetting what she said. And she's always saying, 'Now when I was a girl . . .' and bossing me around all the time."

"But, Ellen. It's just the first day. It'll get better. Why when I was a girl, I used to love to go home with Eunice and stay over night. Lilith was your grandmother's dearest friend. She's practically part of the family."

"I'm not going back." I took a gulp of Pepsi.

"Of course you'll go back. You'll go back when you see what came in the mail today."

"What?"

"A check from Eunice for your first week. Fifteen dollars. Post-dated. That means Saturday morning you can put a down payment on your ten-speed."

Lilith Adams and her cat and her smelly old house vanished as I saw myself wheeling my bike down the drive, with Skeet Barclay watching, then slipping my toes into the rat-traps on the pedals and hearing the tires sing as I pedaled down the street.

"You mean . . . this Saturday?"

"I mean this Saturday. The check's in there on the desk. Made out to you. Go see for yourself."

I knew I was being bribed, but sometimes you want something so badly that you'll do anything to get it. I wanted that ten-speed Raleigh.

"You will go back, won't you, dear? You know you promised Eunice, and you . . . well, you . . . certainly wouldn't want to disappoint her. She could have hired someone else . . . someone older. And she did offer you the job first."

My pride was as overwhelming as my wanting.

"Oh, I'll go back. But . . . Skeet and all the kids think she's baby-sitting with me."

Mother glanced up.

"Baby-sitting? Where did they get that idea?"

"I don't know. But he teased me about it."

Mother slipped off the bar stool and went over to the stove. It was going to be stew again.

"Mother?"

"Yes, dear."

"Lilith's not my baby-sitter, is she?"

"Don't you know better than that?"

"Well, how come I don't go over on weekends?"

"Maybelle stops in on weekends."

"Yeah."

"Besides, you're getting paid, aren't you? Go in and see for yourself. The check's there. The letter too."

She tasted the stew, her back toward me.

"You wouldn't kid me, would you, Mom?"

"Ellen. I'm your mother."

I couldn't quite see why that answered my question, but I accepted it along with the Lilith summer and the promise of the Raleigh ten-speed.

The check was on the desk, and the letter too. I *was* a paid companion. I'd remember that when Mrs. Adams started bossing me around next time.

"Wasn't that nice of Eunice to send the check so early?" Mother had followed me in from the kitchen, and she sat down at the desk and flipped a clean sheet of paper into the typewriter.

"Mom? Is Mrs. Adams sort of . . . well, you know . . . sort of strange? Funny?"

"Oh no, dear. Not really. Just old. Old people tend to get

childish, forgetful, set in their ways. You have to make allowances. Just do as she says. Humor her.''

"But the day gets so long.''

"You love to read. Take some books along. She has TV, doesn't she? And you can spend the afternoons at the pool or over at the park for tennis. Just let her know where you're going. Sort of keep an eye on each other.''

"I'm a *lady*-sitter, then. It rhymes with *baby*. Baby-sitter, lady-sitter.''

"Yes. It does, doesn't it?''

Mother thumbed through an important-looking book. I don't think she wanted to talk about Lilith Adams and Eunice any more than I wanted to think about going back the next day.

"I'm sure glad I'm not old. I'm never going to get old. I'd rather die first.''

"Oh, don't talk silly.'' Mother creased the book open and began to type. "Now be a dear and go set the table. Your father'll be home soon, and I've got to get this typed for tomorrow.''

I went out to the kitchen and watched Skeet Barclay finish mowing the lawn and wondered why I had to do things I didn't want to do in order to do the things I wanted to do. I'd be glad when I was eighteen and could do only what I wanted to do.

Four more days with Lilith and I had one-tenth of the ten-speed. But I could still hear the Lilith commands. Lilith was a "we" person, if one day were any sample: "*We* should get these fruit jars back down cellar. *We* should check on the rose bushes tomorrow.''

I did not want to be a *"we."* I wanted to be a *"me"*—a me on a ten-speed bicycle speeding down a long road that stretched so far ahead I couldn't begin to see the end.

That night, after finishing my mystery story and listening to a new album, I took a magic marker and drew a big red X through that first Monday.

Forty-nine days to go.

EYE TO EYE

FOR THE NEXT FOUR MORNINGS I climbed Blossom Street Hill, padding along bare-footed, the coolness of the night still trapped in the sidewalk. I always stopped at Farley's cottonwood and slipped on my sneakers. Lilith did not approve of bare feet. She hadn't told me why.

The worst thing about Lilith was she never asked questions; she made statements: "You'll like creamed chicken. Slumping in your chair will ruin your back. You are the answer for your own questions."

And she had a set time for everything. At ten, water the plants. Ten-thirty, tidy up the house. Eleven, listen to the TV game show. Eleven-thirty, start lunch. I might as well have been in school. I should hold up my hand, maybe, when I wanted to talk, but Lilith wouldn't get the joke. Besides there was nothing I wanted to say.

The Lilith days were like the ad I saw in an old magazine up in our attic where a girl with an umbrella held a box of salt under her arm. On that box of salt was a picture of another girl, smaller, holding another box of salt, and on that box was another girl, holding another box of salt, and on that box, another girl. It was frightening to think how far it could go. Didn't it ever end?

Skeet Barclay still teased me. Every time he saw me, he didn't say anything. He just grinned and made a motion as if he were rocking a baby.

All that first week I waged a secret war, and Lilith was the enemy. There weren't too many things I could do, but there were little things like biting my nails, cracking my knuckles, and snapping my bubble gum.

By the next Monday, I decided things were going to be different. I would not let any old woman boss me around as if she were my baby-sitter.

I would spend the whole afternoon at the pool.

"Wish I had my bike. It'd take me only five minutes to get there." I narrowed my eyes and smiled.

"Don't squint. Where is your bicycle?"

"I don't have it yet. I'm getting it in August." I smiled harder.

She looked past me as she so often did. "Oh. That's interesting. I'm getting new screens for the porch in August. Aluminum. A present?"

"The screens?"

"No, the bicycle. Is it to be a present?"

I stopped smiling. "A present to myself. I'm earning the money."

"Oh."

"Where you getting your screens?"

"Fullerton's Lumber. A present to myself. I earn too, you know. I'm not entirely useless. And I'm certainly perfectly capable of taking care of. . . ."

"Taking care of what? Who?" Skeet's teasing, stupid as it was, began to make sense.

"Whom, not who. Besides, it's what. Screens are what."

"But you said taking care of. . . ."

"Here." She handed me a brown envelope and a small green book. "On your way to swimming, take this to the bank for me and make a deposit. The woman behind the window will know what to do. She'll mark it down in my book. Mind you don't lose it."

"I won't."

"Close the screen door tight."

I did, and ran all the way to the swimming pool. I'd go to the bank on the way back. But that afternoon they were cleaning the pool because the filter broke, so I trudged back up to the bank.

The woman behind the iron bars had on a lot of makeup and wore blue rhinestone glasses. She smiled at me as she took the envelope and the green book. She knew my name even if I didn't know hers.

Then she stopped and frowned. "Oh, Ellen. Lilith forgot to endorse this one check. Why don't you take it back to her to sign it? She can still get it in her account today." She pushed the pink slip back across the marble counter.

I was almost to Lilith's gate before I thought again of the check clutched in my hand. I guess the only reason I looked at it was to find out if sweat had smudged the ink. That's when I saw my mother's name. The check was for thirty dollars, and Mother's signature was at the bottom. And in the little lined space at the left hand edge was my name.

For a minute I thought it was some secret way of giving me the money for the ten-speed. But I knew it wasn't. Mother was paying Lilith to baby-sit.

But Eunice was paying *me*.

Something hot boiled up inside me. I clenched my teeth. I could feel tears behind my eyes and to stop them I made fists of my hands.

Lilith was in the kitchen when I came in. I thrust the check at her. "You forgot to sign it on the back."

She took it and turned away to find a pen in the wicker basket on the counter under the phone. "Did you look at it?"

I wanted, at first, to lie and pretend that I hadn't seen the names, but I was mad. "She's paying you for being my baby-sitter. For taking care of me. Just so you can get a bunch of old screens."

Lilith smiled at me for the first time. "I don't need *old* screens. I've already got *old* screens . . . a whole porch full."

"Well, I'm getting a *new* ten-speed bicycle. Because I'm sitting with you. And Eunice is paying me. Fifteen dollars a week for the rest of the summer. Because you're old. Too old to be by yourself. And . . . and I hate . . . I hate this summer!"

I slammed the screen door and headed for the willow where I watched Lord Jim stalking birds through Lilith's strawberry bed.

Skeet was right. Everyone knew about it but me. All I could think about was his smirky grin and Mother's lie. It wasn't exactly a lie, but she hadn't told me and that was just as bad. And all because of Lilith. She was probably sitting inside her kitchen and laughing at me.

What could I do? What was the worst thing I could do? I thought of everything, from running away to tripping Lilith on the cellar stairs. But the fifteen dollars I had earned already belonged to Neimeyer's. And the bicycle was closer to belonging to me. How many more hours would it take? I tried to add up the time I'd have to spend with Lilith minus the time for her naps or my afternoons at the pool. I couldn't do it without paper and pencil. I tried scratching numbers in the dirt, but the ground was too hard. So I pulled up six of Lilith's strawberry plants.

Then I did think of something. I could collect my fifteen dollars and not do anything. It would be like getting something for free. I could come every day and not talk to Lilith at all, and she wouldn't tell because Lilith was greedy and wanted new screens. She'd never even figure out what was going on.

"Ellen."

I made her call me twice. But maybe it was four o'clock. Lilith didn't need a clock; she could tick off her own time along with duties and commands.

We had tea and cookies, and I didn't talk to her. She didn't talk to me either.

I hated four to five. It was the beginning-to-die time of the day, even if it meant I could leave soon. Even Lord Jim curled up on the back of the sofa and slept the deadly time away.

"You needn't come back next week, you know." Her voice was too soft.

"Back where?"

"You understand. You needn't come back here. The screens can wait another year. Your bicycle too."

She finished her tea and set the cup back so that it banged against the saucer.

She had figured out what I'd been thinking, but did she have to put it into words?

"I didn't mean I hated *you*." The sounds came out before I knew I intended to make them. "I guess it wasn't your idea. And it sure wasn't mine."

"No. Perhaps that's one of the things that is wrong. I've stopped thinking up ideas. Stopped planning my life." She looked straight at me. "I would have made a better plan, you know."

I didn't know. I seldom knew what she was talking about, but this time I felt as if I should. "What kind of plan?"

"How could I know unless I've made it? And do you know something? I'm not sure that I like you any better than you like me. Why should I? Why should either one of us? And why don't you run home? It's almost five."

But I didn't run home. I sat and drank the rest of my tea and ate another cookie.

"What kind of plan should we make?" I had sat all afternoon under the willow trying to think of something. Lilith might have a better idea. After all, she was old.

"We?" She looked down at the pink check that lay on the table, the check that I had never taken back to the bank.

"You and me. You and me is we."

"And whom are we plotting against?"

"Them. Your Eunice and my mother. They didn't tell either one of us the truth and that's why they're them." It was funny to discover that I didn't know something until I'd said it.

"I'm not sure I can be part of that we." Lilith looked past me again and shook her head.

"Well, I don't care. I don't think it was very nice."

"No. It wasn't very nice. It was humiliating. But there are other words for it. Concern. Love. They think they know what's best. We are very vulnerable, you know. You and I. You, because you're so young. I, because I'm so old."

"You'd think a mother would be fair."

"Or a daughter." Lilith got up from the table. "Now it's our move, girl. We may be coming from opposite sides, but we should be able to see eye to eye."

I glanced at the check. "I know. Let's take the money and pretend we didn't know. I'll get my bike that way, and you'll get your screens."

"It could be a secret between us."

"Then, when the summer's over, we can say we knew all along."

Lilith put the cups down on the counter. "That would not be a bad plan. Yes. We can do that. But what about the rest of the forty-four days?"

I wondered how Lilith knew there were forty-four days left.

THE HOUR

THE TRUCE BEGAN the next day. I folded the laundry—Lilith's way—while she "pressed out a few little things here." I "ran outside to play" when Lilith's TV program came on. I took her check back to the bank on my way to the pool.

And after tea, I picked up the cups and the empty cookie dish and stacked them in the sink. It was four again and the last hour stretched ahead. I sat back down and stared out the window.

LILITH BEGAN TO SING.

I wanted to giggle, but I clenched my teeth and concentrated on the willow tree.

The goldenrod is yellow;
The leaves are turning brown.
The trees in apple orchard
With fruit are bending down.

Reedy and nasal, quavering dangerously in the upper range, but strong in the lower, she sounded like an old wood clarinet.

"That's pretty," I managed to say.

But Lilith wasn't finished. The song went on, the tune unchanged, Lilith squeezing the extra words in, taking hasty tucks in the longer syllables to fit the wandering tune.

The gentian's bluest fringes
Are curling in the sun.
In dusty pods, the milkweed
Its hidden silk has spun.

With hardly a pause and no explanation, Lilith launched into a poem, her eyes on the corner of the ceiling above the refrigerator.

There are strange things done in the midnight sun
By the men who moil for gold;
The Arctic trails have their secret tales
That would make your blood run cold;
The Northern Lights have seen queer sights,
But the queerest they ever did see . . . .

Verse after verse rolled forth, and I shivered in that cold Yukon.

"You know it all by heart!" I cried when she was finished.

"Not by heart," Lilith answered. "By head."

"What's the difference?" That was one way I managed to annoy Lilith: by asking dumb questions.

She didn't answer.

"I've got some mending to do. Let's go into the other room. What is that book you've been reading under the willow?"

I didn't know Lilith knew I was reading the hours away.

We sat that afternoon, from four to five, in front of the curtained bay window—Lilith in her swivel rocker, and I on the footstool, and I told her of the mystery story I had finished about a girl detective.

Lilith listened while she searched for a button to match Mr. Cummings's shirt. He lived next door. She'd offered that morning, shouting over the back fence, "Just bring it over and quit complaining."

She listened even as she rattled through her three-pound coffee can, full of all sizes, designs, and shapes of buttons.

"Why don't you sort them out in piles and keep them separate?"

"What would be the fun? This way I always find something I wasn't looking for."

Just when things were going well, Lilith came up with something strange. I chewed on the inside of my cheek.

"Your story. Most interesting. It reminds me." She laid aside Mr. Cummings's shirt, disappeared into her bedroom, and brought back a book. Adjusting her glasses, after breathing on them and rubbing them briskly against her sleeve, she thumbed through the pages.

"The Hound of the Baskervilles by A. Conan Doyle," she announced. "A. Conan Doyle, you see, was a doctor who wrote detective novels while he waited in his office for patients." She began to read. *"Mr. Sherlock Holmes, who was usually very late in the mornings, save upon those not infrequent occasions when he was up all night, was seated at the breakfast table. I stood upon the hearth-rug and picked up the stick which our visitor had left behind him the night before. . . ."*

The minute hand was far past five when Lilith paused in her reading and glanced up at the living room clock. "Oh, it's past the time. Hurry. Run home. I'll call your mother so she won't worry."

"Can we read more tomorrow?"

"By all means. And maybe we can solve the mystery. Two heads ought to be equal to one. Don't you think?"

"I'll think it over tonight," I promised, not realizing I was promising.

"And I will do the same. Don't miss a clue. Sometimes they aren't so easy to recognize."

It didn't occur to me until I was on the way home that Lilith had probably read *The Hound of the Baskervilles* before.

The rest of the weeks, the hour between four and five sealed the truce. We took turns, after the Sherlock Holmes, trying to surprise each other.

One day it was the Saint-Saens piano concerto by Lilith. That was not very good.

"But the orchestra is supposed to play those in-between parts," she explained. "Next time I'll try the Cesar Franck. I can do that . . . I think."

The poem writing was much better. One week we wrote poems about anything we wanted to, and then we read them aloud to each other. I read mine first.

A POEM FOR LORD JIM
He sits fierce and quite in the sun
His whiskers flick, his face is grim.
Lord Jim thinks of mice and birds,
He purrs and we don't know his words.
I used to be afraid of him
Like an ugly bird perched on the end of a tree limb.
Now we sit for hours and hours
While mice run and laugh behind the flowers.

"That was rather good," Lilith said, nodding slowly. "But let me hear those first two lines again."

He sits fierce and quite in the sun
His whiskers flick, his face is grim.

"Why don't you try *glum* at the end of that first line?"
I read again:

He sits fierce and quite in the sun
His whiskers flick, his face is glum.

"Much better. *Quiet* is spelled q-u-i-e-t."

LILITH'S POEM was much better than mine. A little hard to understand in places, but the words went together in such a nice way, I didn't really have to understand.

A POEM FOR LORD JIM AND ELLEN
How do you see yourselves, my dears,
In this, my quiet garden?
Does sunlight magnify your fears
Or do my eyes? I ask your pardon,
But you are much braver than you think,
Or you might be, if you tried;
It's fearing life that forms the link
Twixt child and cat—twixt lived and died.
You with wide, round silent eyes
Crouch beneath the threat of days;
You sense, not know, the hour that flies
And brings the end to sunlit ways.
I wish you peace, my little friends,
And all the bravery living lends.

Almost grudgingly I had to admit the days did go faster after we started doing things from four to five. One day we made up a new language called "Lilellenish" . . . with new names for things and new verbs, only Lilith called the verbs "doing" words and the adjectives "painting" words.

Hedral stood for man; *regan* was woman. Lilith made up *regan*. She said she "borrowed" it from Shakespeare and it really meant queen, "which is what every woman is or can become."

Clawfy was cat. That was mine. *Toots* meant birds. That was mine too. For several afternoons, and mornings too, we talked in Lilellenish, and when Maybelle, Lilith's friend, visited one day, Lilith said to me, "Clawfy gomoranda meeki," which meant in Lilellenish, "The cat wants out."

And Maybelle said, "What are you teaching the kid? Welsh, for God's sake?"

But Lilith didn't tell Maybelle. She avoided the question completely and changed the subject. From that day on Lilellenish became our other secret. Lilith could always make up the best sentences, though, or at least her sentences always came out sounding the funniest. When she spoke Lilellenish, her voice went up and down as if it were a real language.

My best sentence was "Squeeby cush moo." It meant, "I love you." But there was never any reason to use it . . . except for Lord Jim.

One Friday, Lilith taught me how to draw fence posts that got smaller and smaller, until they looked as if they disappeared off the page.

"That is perspective. It is a difficult thing to master. But it's necessary for seeing . . . for seeing telephone poles, trees, corn in rows, or whatever is lined up against you."

That night, up in my room, I tried to draw the things that were lined up against me: Skeet, Mother, Eunice, and . . . and Lilith, but I couldn't line up people as well as fence posts.

THE WEDNESDAYS

WEDNESDAY AFTERNOONS at Lilith's were reserved for three-handed bridge with Maybelle and Grace. Sometimes Friday afternoons too if the day were dull and overcast.

"Grace can't handle dark days," Lilith explained.

"I'll go to the pool when they come."

"Grace doesn't always remember what day it is. Run up to her house and tell her it's Wednesday."

Sometimes I thought Lilith was hard of hearing. Other times I wasn't sure. She had a habit of hearing what she wanted to hear, and this left me wondering if I'd really said what I'd said or just thought I'd said it.

"I'll ring up Maybelle."

"Why can't you call Grace too?"

"Grace takes her phone off the hook after eleven."

"Eleven in the morning?"

"Eleven in the morning. Now run along."

If Lilith was strange, Grace was weird. I never knew what to expect of Grace. One time she might fling open her front door so hard it banged against the iron doorstop, clasp me in her thin arms with "Oh, Lovey. It's you. Lilith's Little One," and step backwards down the long hall, tugging me into the house.

"Precious one. Little one. You need nourishment," she would repeat over and over as she swayed out toward the kitchen, her faded blue chiffon robe streaming out behind. She would return, bursting through the swinging kitchen door, with one lone ginger snap—always a ginger snap so dry I couldn't bite it. Grace, on those days, would talk a crazy jumble of words and half phrases.

"Oh, little sweetheart, you must eat. Eat . . . eat to grow. To grow big. Big." Then her face would change and she'd look angry. "But don't believe them. They lie. They always lie. You don't grow big. You grow old. You think you're growing big, but one day you wake up and you're not big at all. You're only old. Old."

I never knew what to do or what to say. I'd sit on the edge of the hard sofa and suck on the dry ginger snap until it grew mushy enough so I could chew it.

Once Grace flew to the grand piano in the front parlor, tore off the fringed scarf, and played and sang a funny song about Sad, Sad Sally in Our Back Alley. Lilith would never have approved of the words. But Grace was exciting. It was like a dream where everything changed so quickly you couldn't remember the next morning what happened.

Other times Grace might open the door just a crack, the night chain still on, and stare out with glazed eyes, mumbling as if she had a bad cold, "Who are you? What do you want?"

Grace smelled funny too, like rotting apples mixed in with lavender perfume.

"Is Grace rich?" I asked Lilith one morning. "Dad says if you're rich enough you can act as crazy as you want to."

Lilith, stirring up a cake, missed a beat with the wooden spoon and peered across the kitchen.

"Grace is old money."

"What's that mean?"

"Means she's always been rich."

"Are you old money too?"

"No," Lilith almost chuckled. "Poor. Land poor. But you can be rich in other ways, you know, besides bank accounts and fourteen-room brick mansions on Oak Drive."

"Maybe," but I was not convinced. "Has Grace always been your friend?"

"I've known Grace since we were girls. We weren't really friends then. The years brought us together."

Lilith had forgotten the cake and was looking out the kitchen window.

"At seventeen, Grace picked her friends. At seventy-seven, she accepts them. You see, when we were young, Grace was everything I wanted to be. But I've had happiness in life that Grace has missed. Things do have a way of leveling out . . . if you live long enough."

Lilith resumed her stirring.

Maybelle was just as strange as Grace. Maybelle always appeared for the three-handed bridge in a hat—a *big* hat. Without a hat, she towered above Lilith and dwarfed little Grace, but with a hat she could hardly get in Lilith's front door without stooping.

My job on Wednesday afternoons was to help Lilith serve the refreshments.

"Good for you. Teach you some social graces."

I didn't know what "social graces" were, but I thought it must have something to do with Grace and being rich, so I always watched Grace very carefully.

"Take the cups into the dining room, now. Mind you don't drop them. Grace hand painted them, you know."

I knew. I heard the same words every Wednesday. Besides, I had been at Grace's often enough. Her dining room was wall-to-wall china: bluebirds, electric blue, perched on green branches; strawberries redder than real, caught in a circle of gold; tulips, egg-yolk yellow; and grapes, intense purple. Wherever I looked were the painted china circles: dinner plates, dessert plates, bread and butter plates. And even under the molding were painted cups hung on little brass holders—all around the dining room like a necklace.

"It's the one thing Grace learned in life: to paint china. It fits her, somehow." Lilith's voice drifted away.

Only Maybelle and Lilith got coffee on bridge afternoons.

"Grace brings her own," Lilith told me.

I'd pour coffee for Maybelle, who barked out a "thank you" that sounded more like an order, and then for Lilith, who merely nodded.

Grace filled her own china cup from a silver thermos, and her cup was empty long before either Maybelle or Lilith had finished theirs.

That afternoon, I saw Grace make a fluttering movement to reach her thermos beside Lilith. Perched on the footstool, I watched Lilith's hand moving under the table across her own broad lap to touch Grace's knee and pat it gently. Grace's hand flew back to reassemble her cards, and the game went on.

"You reneged, Grace!" Maybelle's bellow interrupted the silence of the game. "You had a trump all along. I played trump three tricks back."

I didn't understand, but I knew Grace had done something wrong.

Lilith, collecting the deck for the next deal, brushed Grace's arm, accidentally it looked, drawing her attention from Maybelle. "She didn't mean to, Maybelle. Did you, Grace?"

"The spade was behind my heart. I didn't notice."

"You couldn't see a spade if it had a handle and was stuck in your hand. Why don't you pay attention to the game?"

Lilith motioned toward the buffet with a tiny nod. I knew I was to pass the brownies—chocolate-frosted brownies arranged like a fan on the strawberry china plate. Mistakes could be forgiven if Maybelle had a "little something to munch on."

The next hand Grace must have made an even bigger mistake, for Maybelle threw her cards down on the table and said, "I give up. Grace, how could you possibly bid a grand slam in hearts with only three hearts and a string of worthless diamonds?"

"My diamonds were mixed in with my hearts."

I passed the brownies again.

Promptly at quarter to five, Grace's limousine pulled up, filling the narrow side drive. Grace lived only three blocks from Lilith, but she never walked over.

"Can I drop you off someplace, Maybelle dear?" Grace offered, the bridge game forgotten.

That the tiny Grace could drop the huge Maybelle anywhere made me start to giggle, but a warning glance from Lilith stopped that.

Maybelle declined the offer to ride that day, and after Grace was gone, she and Lilith sat sipping the last of the coffee, talking in low whispers so I couldn't hear and shaking their heads.

I walked home with Maybelle. Maybelle lived on up the block from Lilith. I walked. Maybelle talked between gulps of air.

"Walking . . . best exercise in the world. You youngsters . . . don't do enough of it. . . . You're going to turn out to be a pack of weaklings. 'Civilized man has built a coach . . . but has lost the use of . . . his feet.' That's Emerson, child."

I didn't know anyone named Emerson, but I nodded. I wondered if Maybelle really liked to walk as much as she claimed, or if she pretended she did because she didn't have a car and Grace did. I decided I'd ask Lilith about that the next day, and I wanted to ask her about Grace too.

And I did, the very next morning.

"Does Grace drink?"

The quick bread was flowing into the narrow tin baking dish, prodded by swift darts of the wooden spoon held firmly in Lilith's hand.

"The secret of making quick bread is to mix it quick and bake it quick. Before the baking soda loses its strength. I suppose that's why it's called quick bread. Don't you think?"

Perhaps Lilith had not heard my question above the clatter of the spoon, but I thought she had.

"Does she?"

"Does she what?"

"Does she drink?"

"Whom are you talking about?"

"Grace. Does she drink?"

Lilith slipped the quick bread into the oven, adjusting the temperature knob carefully. "Just a touch below 350 degrees should do it, and we'll have quick bread for lunch."

I knew I was not to ask again, but I had to know. Maybelle told me once, "If you want to know something, ask."

Lilith, on the kitchen stool, eyed the oven as if guarding the bread from any catastrophe.

I leaned over the stove and looked straight into her eyes, daring her to answer.

"All right." Lilith wiped the steam from her glasses on the corner of her apron. "She drinks."

Somehow, hearing it was much worse than thinking it. Lilith's house was exciting when Grace was around, and now the wild magic of Grace wasn't magic at all. I studied the leaf pattern in Lilith's kitchen linoleum.

"You have to know Grace to understand. We all have our crutches."

"Why does she do it?"

Lilith wiped a finger mark off the oven door handle with her apron. "Grace is one of the gentle ones. Too fragile. She breaks easily."

I straightened up and felt bigger and wiser and more knowing than Lilith could ever be.

"Well, I think it's awful."

"Life is a razor edge to Grace. She thinks she should be able to walk that edge. Sometimes she does, for a moment or two. And who's to say a few moments balancing on the edge isn't worth a life of trying?"

"She shouldn't drink."

"No. I don't suppose she should."

"If it's a crutch, she should throw it away."

"You judge like a child . . . or a reformer."

"I'm *not* a child!"

"Then you must be a reformer."

I did not like the sound of the word or the tone of Lilith's voice.

"Now Maybelle has her hats. To make her taller."

Lilith was up to her old tricks, trying to lure me away from Grace.

"Oh, I thought she wore those hats because she's so old-fashioned. Maybelle's tall enough already."

"Oh no. You're very wrong. Maybelle is tiny. Very tiny indeed. And very frightened."

"And Grace?"

I would get Lilith back to Grace.

"Now, Grace. . . ."

"Is she afraid, too?"

"Yes. Grace is afraid."

"Of what?"

"Of growing old . . . and ugly. Of being alone. Of having to look at herself. Of living."

Lilith moved to the screen door and watched Lord Jim making his way along the top of the picket fence.

"Does everybody have crutches?"

"I suspect so."

"You too?"

Lilith crossed over to the sink and turned the faucet on full force into the mixing bowl.

"Well? Do you? Have a crutch?"

"Only Lord Jim . . . and . . . and. . . ."

I didn't really hear the last word. I thought she had said, "And . . . *you*." I wasn't sure, and somehow I couldn't ask. Lilith was bent over the dish pan, clattering the silverware in a foam of suds.

I picked up my book and went out to the willow.

YELLOW-CRESTED BLACKBIRDS

"LIL! THE YELLOW-CIRCLED blackbirds are back! Down in Wenzel's Swamp. Where is that woman?"

Mr. Cummings, like a late summer grasshopper, appeared at the back screen door.

I had seen the old Mercury weave into the drive. Like a miracle, the car slid around the turn with only one wheel catching the curb.

Nothing was safe when Mr. Cummings was loose in a car.

"He's several years older than I, you know," Lilith had explained. "But he's a nice old gentleman. Some people you talk to. Mr. Cummings, you talk with and about."

"About what?"

"Birds, of course. They're his hobby. Hobbies keep a person alive."

"We haven't had yellow-circled blackbirds around here for over fifteen years," Mr. Cummings explained as Lilith held the screen door open. "They're down in Wenzel's Swamp, Lil. Or did I say that? My memory isn't as good as it used to be."

"Oh, Mr. Cummings, there's nothing wrong with your memory. Sometimes I think you remember too much." I'd seen Lilith smile before, but I'd never heard her laugh like that.

"Now, Lil. Some things it doesn't pay to forget. But about the birds. There's a whole flock of them. Yellow-circled, mind you."

"I believe they are called yellow-crested, Mr. Cummings. Not yellow-circled."

"Same difference. We called them yellow-circled when I was a kid. But come along. I've got the car out. I'll drive you down."

"How nice. To think of us. We'd love to go. But let me set this bread dough on the back of the stove. Why don't you sit down and have a blueberry muffin with honey before we go?"

"Don't mind if I do," he laughed as he pulled out a chair and rested his elbows on the table. Lilith didn't even frown. She never let me put my elbows on the table.

"Ellen. Fetch the honey from the top shelf."

I obeyed.

I didn't like Mr. Cummings and I couldn't understand why Lilith did. She acted comfortable with him, different from the way she was with Maybelle or Grace—even me, after our truce. It was as if they had a special language that didn't use words.

"Still got that old flea bag around?" Mr. Cummings chuckled as the muffin crumbled halfway to his mouth, spilling honey on his pant leg.

"Now that's an unfair question." But Lilith didn't sound angry. "If I say *yes,* I'm conceding that he is a flea bag. And if I say *no,* I'm not only telling an untruth, but I'm still calling my

Lord Jim a flea bag. That makes it a loaded question and an unfair question."

"Well," the old man drawled, "let's put it this way. When are you going to get rid of that dang cat so I can marry you?"

Marry Lilith! Mr. Cummings wasn't just silly, he was sick. Old people didn't get married. I waited to hear Lilith laugh.

"You'll have to take us both. I'm not getting rid of that cat, Mr. Cummings. I've told you before."

"Did you say *not,* Mrs. Adams?"

"I said *not.* A categorical not."

"Did you hear that, Jim, you bird gulper? A categorical not. Not only standing in the way of romance, you old scavenger, you're living here with a categorical not over your head."

On the rug, Lord Jim yawned, his tongue flipping up in a curl.

I didn't know what a categorical knot was, but I could see Lord Jim, if Mr. Cummings were to have his way, with a categorical knot tied around his neck, attached to the clothesline post and never allowed to roam the backyards again.

"Keep in mind, Mr. Cummings, there is such a thing as the balance of nature. You're just doing your humble part, aren't you, Lord Jim, to balance nature?"

Lord Jim let out a rasping meow.

Mr. Cummings winked at me as if I were in on his joke, but I was still puzzling out the categorical knot. The *cat* I could understand easily enough. The *gore* sounded like the Sherlock Holmes story. But *knots* . . . knots were . . . cruel.

I looked straight at Mr. Cummings, unsmiling, and vowed I would untie any knot he ever dared tie around Lord Jim's throat.

"Seriously, Lil, you really ought to get rid of that cat. Gobbled up a robin the other day. In *my* backyard, too, it was."

"That's why it's going to stay *your* backyard. Cats may not understand lot lines, but I do. This is a fine house and Jim and I are comfortable here." As she so often did, Lilith sounded as if she were talking about one thing and saying something else.

"But how can I lure birds into my backyard with this Jungle Jim eating them as fast as I spot them?"

"Now, Mr. Cummings. You can't set aside a Garden of Eden over there on your lot with just flowers and birds and bees."

"Not with a Lilith Adams and a cat next door. That's for darn sure."

I escaped to the living room and the swivel rocker. They would keep on as long as the muffins lasted, and Lilith had set out three on the blue willow plate.

I would read. I had brought a new book along, about a prince who came to the Sahara Desert.

> The fox gazed at the little prince, for a long time.
>
> "Please—tame me!" he said.
>
> "I want to, very much," the little prince replied. "But I have not much time. I have friends to discover, and a great many things to understand."
>
> "One only understands the things that one tames," said the fox. "Men have no more time to understand anything. . . . If you want a friend, tame me. . . ."
>
> "What must I do, to tame you?" asked the little prince.

"Ellen."

I read to the bottom of the page before I answered.

"Yeah?"

"Come along. Mr. Cummings is ready."

"I'm not going."

I did not hear Lilith come into the living room, but I felt her standing beside me. I did not look up. I focused on the buckle of her belt.

"You're not going?"

It was the gentleness of the question that made my eyes leap up to her face and then down again to the belt buckle.

"No," I said.

"Why not?"

"He's . . . so old. And so dumb."

"Old? By what measure? By a clock? A calendar?"

"Just old."

"I tell you, in the pure joy of living, in the pure joy of loving living things, he's far younger than you."

"He's eighty."

"Ellen, I'm not one for long arguments."

Lilith was not joking, I knew. I was not joking either.

"Yes, ma'am," I managed and shifted my eyes to Lilith's sturdy brown oxfords.

"Then state your case, and I'll state mine."

"I don't care about any yellow-crested blackbirds."

"Don't you care about dear Mr. Cummings?"

How could I answer? I wanted to say, as Lilith had just said, "That's an unfair question. A loaded question." So I lied. It was easier.

"Yeah. I guess so."

"We'll go see the yellow-crested blackbirds, then." Lilith turned and headed for the door.

Something made me unfold my legs, throw the book aside, and follow.

I wanted to kick Lilith's prized antique wardrobe as I clomped by. I wanted to scream. I hated the power Lilith had, and I hated myself more for giving in.

Lilith climbed in the front seat with Mr. Cummings, and I sulked down in the empty back seat that smelled like a basement full of old newspapers.

A drive with Mr. Cummings was equal to sixteen roller coaster rides. Every start, every lurch, every turn was a threat, and even though Mr. Cummings acted as if he were in command, I knew differently, as I tossed and tumbled about in the back seat.

Didn't Lilith Adams know she was endangering a child's life in forcing me to go along?

"What a lovely idea this was, Mr. Cummings. To take us to

the swamp on such a beautiful morning! Don't you agree, Ellen?"

Why couldn't Lilith be fair? I had come along, hadn't I? Without too much fuss. What more did she want? But I knew. She wanted me to be "cheerful and sunny." Those were Lilith's favorite words, "cheerful and sunny." I would do what Lilith said, but no one could make me be cheerful and sunny.

"I say, Ellen, isn't this nice?"

"Isn't this nice?" I parroted.

"Spunky one, ain't she?" Mr. Cummings whispered across to Lilith. "Remember when Pearl refused to go up and get her diploma in the eighth grade 'cause they had to wear white dresses?"

"It wasn't that Pearl wouldn't wear a white dress, Mr. Cummings, if you remember. It was that Fayetta Reed couldn't afford one, and Fayetta was going to stay home."

"Yeah. Guess that was the way it was. Always looking out for the underdog, Pearl was."

I leaned forward to hear their words. They were talking about my grandmother. It didn't make any difference that it happened years and years ago; it was *my* grandmother. I hadn't even known her. She'd died before I was born, but just the same, what right did they have to talk about her?

And then I started thinking that if my grandmother—Grandmother Pearl—were alive, she might look something like Lilith, and not like the picture on Mom's dresser. Did that mean that my grandmother would have been bossy and forgetful and click her false teeth and talk about the old days and insist on doing things her way and correct me all the time and claim there was only one way to fold bath towels and . . . ?

Mr. Cummings slammed on the brakes and I was bounced against the front seat and back again into the back seat. Lilith pretended not to notice the abrupt stop.

"Now come on down here with me," Mr. Cummings directed as he scrambled through the waist-high grass that ringed the swamp. "Get down here in the grass and don't move. Here's where I saw them earlier this morning."

At first I felt foolish, squatting in the grass with Mr. Cummings and Lilith. I could imagine what Skeet Barclay would say. Mr. Cummings took out his binoculars from the case over his shoulder and scanned the sky.

The air was fresh and still with only the low hum of gnats circling above our heads. I was getting bored when there was a flutter, and a cattail stalk bent under the weight of a delicate bird, black—so black the wings were almost purple—and with a dainty yellow marking, like golden dust, running from the beak across the crown into the ruff.

No one moved. No one said a word. Mr. Cummings sat poised, the binoculars halfway to his eyes. Lilith, her hand shading her eyes, loomed above me like an ancient statue.

And somehow the bird was important to me, too. Ordinary blackbirds I knew. And red-winged blackbirds. But yellow-crested blackbirds. The name itself was beautiful. And for the first time, too, I thought Lilith looked beautiful with the morning sun shining through her white hair and the puff of breeze blowing out the stray strands like silvered silk.

I don't know how long we sat there in Wenzel's Swamp, but another bird joined the first and then another and another. I do know that when we got up to leave, my left leg was numb and prickly, and that Mr. Cummings helped Lilith along as if he were as big and strong as she. And she let him.

No one said much on the way home, and Mr. Cummings drove real slow.

THE PEARL RING

THE FLOOR TILE COOLED my bare feet as we pushed open the glass doors of Parson's General Store.

"Where are your shoes?" Lilith frowned down at my feet.

"Forgot them."

"Of course," she sniffed. Lilith could use the same words to mean so many different things. Sometimes her "of course" was a gentle pat. This one was not.

"I don't see what's wrong with bare feet."

"Nasty habit."

I didn't feel like fighting the battle for my liberation. Shopping with Lilith was enough to tackle for one morning.

Shopping with Lilith took forever.

"I look before I buy." And Lilith did.

Parson's Store was dimly lit, dark enough to make mysterious nooks at the far ends of each aisle.

I walked around the counters stacked with cards of shiny buttons and rolls of bright fabrics piled high against the wall. Mrs. Parsons was talking with Lilith, her lips opening and closing, tongue flicking like a frog. The sound of their voices blended with the whirring of the ceiling fan.

I ran my fingers over the things on the next counter: pens, paste, glue, erasers, tablets with an eagle on the cover, stacks of notebook paper sealed under plastic. There was something fascinating and, at the same time, forbidding about the displays. I moved to the back of the store, then turned and began the circuit back toward Lilith. I liked the way the store smelled: a mixture of cleaning compound, moth balls, perfume, powder, and leather. I moved past the lipstick, deodorants, face powder, and lotions shelved behind sliding glass doors and stopped to gaze at the medical supplies.

The medical supplies blended into the jewelry: necklaces of dangling gold pendants, earrings clipped to tiny squares of cardboard piled high in a wicker basket, compacts, souvenir spoons, and *rings*.

The rings nestled in styrofoam slots, displayed on an octagonal case that revolved when I touched it with my finger. And there, among the fake rubies and too-green emeralds was a pearl ring. It was white as fresh milk, perfect as a tear drop—so simple, so out of place, I felt that I alone had discovered it.

Without thinking, I reached out, slipped the pearl ring from its slot, and jammed it down into the pocket of my shorts. It felt cool in my palm and the pearl itself smooth against my fingertips. I moved quickly away, my hand thrust firmly down into my pocket. The ring slipped on to my finger. It was just the right size.

It was only after I passed the racks of candy bars and

chewing gum that I realized what I had done. By then it was too late—too late to put the ring back into the styrofoam slot on the rack.

I skipped up to Lilith, my fingers curled tightly around the band in my pocket, clenching my teeth to hold back the glee I felt inside.

Lilith peered down at me.

"Shall we go now?" Her voice sounded low and intimate.

"I don't care." I tried not to appear too eager.

Lilith pushed through the glass door, and I, my pocket full of triumph, followed the broad back out into the hot, dusty street.

"That Mrs. Parsons is a fine woman. Manages that big store all by herself since her husband died. A fine, fine woman."

I felt the pearl ring, suddenly a hot band around my finger. I swallowed with effort, but an ugly taste stuck in my throat. I ran my tongue around the outside of my lips.

"Where are we going now?" I tried to sound enthusiastic.

"I thought we'd go over there on that bench in the square and rest a bit before we start home. Would you like that?"

I could think of nothing I would like less, but I forced my head to nod. I trailed half a step behind Lilith, keeping my right hand in my pocket, just out of Lilith's sight. As Lilith turned to sit down, I managed to slip the ring off.

The streets were empty. I would have welcomed anyone—anyone who might at least bring forth a comment or a story from Lilith to fill the awkward pause.

"Oh, my. It is nice to sit down, isn't it?"

"We could've gone down to Reed's and sat and had a coke."

"We can do that too . . . after we rest a spell."

I did not feel like resting. I felt like running. I kept seeing the big sign across the street: Parson's General Store. I could hardly keep my legs still, and I didn't know what to do with my hands. I folded them in my lap, then rubbed my sweaty palms against my bare knees. I twisted as the bench seat burned the back of my legs. I ran my hand through my hair.

Lilith sat beside me and gazed across the street with a faraway look.

"Sure hot, isn't it?"

Lilith nodded.

"We going to sit here very long?"

"Not too long."

I rocked back and forth, my arms clutching my waist.

"Almost the hottest day we've had, I bet."

Lilith did not answer.

I could feel the pearl in my pocket, a soft bump against my leg. I glanced down, carefully, to see if the bump showed, and Lilith chose that very second to turn toward me.

I smiled, but Lilith did not smile back.

What was she waiting for? Surely we had sat long enough to be rested by now. The silences grew longer. They flowed over and around me like the heat from the sidewalk. I tried to think of something to say, but for the first time I was speechless. I couldn't even think of something mean.

Then out of a silence that I was positive was never going to end came Lilith's voice, soft but heavy with a funny sadness.

"You wanted it very much, didn't you?"

I felt my lips tremble and my breath slipped out in two gasps that I couldn't control.

"Wanted? What?" I needed time to think.

"Don't make me say it for you."

I felt the lump in my pocket.

"Maybe," Lilith said, "we should just start at the end instead of at the beginning. Shall we?"

I moved my lips to form words, but no sound came.

"We can walk back across the street and tell Mrs. Parsons."

"We?"

A cool breeze ruffled my hair.

"What . . . what'll we say?" My voice shook like Grace's.

"We'll say we want to return some merchandise—merchandise we have not paid for."

"Will you say it for us?"

"No. You will say it. It will not be too difficult. It will be hard, but not too difficult. Shall we go now?"

I was not ready to go, but I knew it was the time.

"It will not take long," Lilith assured me.

I couldn't make my feet match Lilith's long strides. I tagged behind, wishing desperately Lilith would walk a little bit slower. The glass door opened before Lilith's determined push. The smell of the store sickened me. Mrs. Parsons loomed behind the cash register, a huge face full of eyes, as Lilith led me by the hand up to the check-out counter.

"You're back, Mrs. Adams?" Mrs. Parson's voice sounded as if she were anticipating another sale. "Did you forget something?"

"Yes. We forgot something. We forgot something very important."

"Well, then," Mrs. Parsons brightened. "What can I do to help you?"

"Ellen wishes to tell you something."

Ellen did not wish to tell Mrs. Parsons anything, but Lilith squeezed my hand.

I stared at the yardstick, nailed to the edge of the counter, focused my eyes on the number 18 halfway down its length, and drew in a big breath. I could hardly make the words come, and I didn't know what I was going to say until I heard my own voice. "We . . . I mean . . . I . . . took a pearl ring. . . . I want to give it back. I won't do it again."

I should have chosen the words more carefully. They sounded so childish. I was ashamed of the words, ashamed of how they were making me feel, ashamed of the way my knees were shaking, ashamed of the way my hand trembled as I pulled the ring out of my pocket and placed it on the counter.

I felt Mrs. Parsons's eyes on me. Lilith let go of my hand.

"You may go now, Ellen," Lilith spoke softly and very slowly, "and put it back where you found it."

I picked up the ring from the counter without looking at Mrs. Parsons, and walked down the long, long aisle to the jewelry counter. I reached out and pushed the pearl ring back into the empty slot.

"Now, Mrs. Parsons," Lilith's voice was familiar again. "I wonder if you would have the time to show us what you have in *rings*. Would you happen to have anything in birthstones?"

"Yes, indeed we do, Mrs. Adams." Mrs. Parsons scurried down the aisle. "We have them for every month of the year. What month did you want?"

"June," Lilith answered.

"June?" Mrs. Parsons turned toward Lilith, puzzled. "That would be. . . ." She consulted a chart. "That's what I thought. Pearl."

I shriveled with shame.

"That is precisely right, Mrs. Parsons."

"Gemini, isn't it?"

"That's right. Gemini," repeated Lilith. "Gemini, the twins. We are Gemini, Ellen and I. Children of June. I suppose you could say we are twins . . . except for a few years."

Mrs. Parsons slipped the same pearl ring from the same styrofoam slot in the octagonal display and held it out for Lilith to examine.

I could not watch. I looked at the floor and hastily counted the red spots in the blocks of linoleum. There were twenty-three red spots in every green tile.

"We'll take it," Lilith said.

Mrs. Parsons hurried up the aisle. Lilith unsnapped her purse, took out her billfold, and pulled out two crisp one-dollar bills.

"Ellen, you pay Mrs. Parsons for the ring. It costs one dollar and seventy-nine cents plus tax."

Outside on the street, as I carried the pearl ring in its dainty white box, Lilith announced, "The ring is yours, Ellen. It is your birthstone."

I stifled an urge to encircle Lilith's waist and bury my head in the soft folds of her dress.

Instead I carefully stepped over every crack in the sidewalk and sang frantically to myself:

Step on a crack
Break your mother's back
Step on a crack
Break your mother's back
Step on a crack
Break Lilith's back

And I didn't step on a single crack.

Lilith never mentioned the pearl ring again. Nor did she ever ask why.

A PAUSE

THE DAYS RAN TOGETHER: steel-blue mornings, sand-gold afternoons. Fall's only hint came in Lilith's song, a song she hummed without knowing she hummed. A song sung for just the singing.

The golden rod is yellow;
The leaves are turning brown.
The trees in apple orchard
With fruit are bending down.

But fall and the end of the summer and my ten-speed Raleigh still seemed so far away.

"Next week we get a vacation," Lilith announced one Friday. "I'm going to visit Eunice. She called early this morning. I'm

flying out for a few days. Then, when I get back, I plan to spend
the rest of the time with Grace. She's not been sleeping well
lately. She needs someone around."

"What about me?"

My first thought was that I'd lose fifteen dollars and that
would set my payments back on the ten-speed.

"I've talked it over with your mother this morning. Before
she left for school. After all, I am a baby-sitter, remember? And
don't you have a friend spending the summer up at some
cabin?"

"Yeah. Fran."

"Say *yes,* not *yeah.*"

"Yes."

"That's better. Well, you get to spend the week up there.
What's the matter? You don't look too thrilled about it."

"I was just wondering."

"Wondering what?"

"About my pay."

"Oh, yes. Your pay."

"And your pay too."

"It's to be a paid vacation, I understand. Eunice and your
mother—they arranged it."

I really wanted to hide, so Lilith couldn't see me. I felt like
shouting . . . like screaming . . . like running. I was free. Free
for a whole week. I wouldn't have to Lilith-sit. I hugged myself to
hold in the wonderful feeling. I picked up my book and ran into
the living room. Sometimes I got tired of the willow and read in
Lilith's swivel rocker that stood in the far corner near the piano.
It could be turned so it faced the corner, its high back shutting
out the rest of the world.

I heard Lilith in the kitchen, singing her same old song, only
now it was more lively and the words bounced merrily through
the tune.

The gentian's bluest fringes
Are curling in the sun.

Then she was talking on the phone to Maybelle: "I'm off on a vacation. For a whole week. Isn't that wonderful?"

She hung up and shouted to me, "I'm going over to Mr. Cummings's. I'll just be a minute."

But she stayed nearly an hour. I decided as I sat there, thumbing through my book, that Lilith was just as happy getting rid of her baby-sitting job as I was my lady-sitting chore. Somehow it was all right for me to escape from Lilith, but I didn't like having her be so happy escaping from me.

Lilith began packing that afternoon, right after lunch. She could have waited until I went home. She "rinsed out a few little things," laid out her "basic blue," mixed up a "batch of banana bread" for Eunice. "Banana bread was a must around here when your mother and Eunice were girls." She tugged down her old suitcase and lined the bottom with the latest edition of the local newspaper. "Eunice likes to keep track."

"It's always so exciting to be going someplace," she commented as she swept through the living room into her bedroom, and I, in the swivel rocker, pretended I didn't hear.

"I'll breathe in life again. Eunice has tickets to a play for one night and a concert the next. They're doing a Copland program."

"Oh, really?" I had never heard of Copland.

"And I dearly love to fly. You feel like you're really going someplace when you fly. Mr. Cummings is taking me to the airport, the dear soul. We'll be leaving at six-thirty."

"In the morning?"

"In the morning."

"When does your plane leave?"

"At nine."

"But it only takes a half hour to get to the airport."

"I know. Still it's better to be early. Then we won't have to hurry."

"But the way Mr. Cummings drives. . . ."

"Mr. Cummings is a fine driver—if he takes his time. He's most cautious."

I wanted to say, "Sure, if he'd look at the road," but I didn't.

"Maybe I'll send you a postcard. Would you like that? Write down your address up there at that lake, wherever you're going."

"I will. After a while."

"And what will you be doing up at that cabin?"

"Oh, fun things. I was up there once last summer. There's a big amusement park with a roller coaster and stuff. Just like a carnival. And Fran's folks have a real neat inboard and she's going to teach me to water ski. She promised. And there's five pizza huts and a fun house and an arcade with pinball machines."

"Oh, really?"

"I could send you a card, too. If I had your address."

"Why don't you do that? There's nothing more fun than getting mail when you're away from home."

Lilith was so busy we didn't have time for our four-to-five hour.

"Who's going to take care of Lord Jim?" I asked as we finished our afternoon tea and I retrieved my book and got ready to go home.

"Mr. Cummings."

"Mr. Cummings? But he hates cats."

"He's doing it for me. He knows what Lord Jim means to me. Mr. Cummings is a very understanding person."

"He won't hurt Lord Jim, will he?"

"Mr. Cummings would not hurt anything or anyone in this whole, wide, wonderful world."

I grinned up at Lilith. "Is that a categorical not?"

"Yes, as a matter of fact, it is."

I knew good-byes and thank-yous and such were a part of "good breeding," as Lilith told me so many times, but I didn't know how to say good-bye, and I didn't see why I had to. I knew I'd be right back in the same old rut of a schedule the very next week after my vacation.

If it had been Skeet or Fran, I'd just say, "So long. Be seeing you," but I didn't think that would pass Lilith standards.

"Well, you'd better run on home and pack now. Your mother said you'd be leaving in the morning too."

"Yeah. I mean yes. I'm going now."

"Do enjoy yourself, Ellen."

"I will." I tried to make it sound convincing, but it didn't come out that way. "You too."

"I shall, Ellen."

FRAN DIDN'T EVEN HAVE a clock up at her cabin. We ate whenever we were hungry, stayed up as late as we wanted, slept till noon, and went barefoot all the time. Every afternoon we went to the beach and every night Fran's older sister took us to the amusement park. Fran's dad ran the whole thing, and we rode the bumper cars, roller coaster, loop-the-loop—all for free.

One night the ferris wheel stopped, and Fran and I were stuck at the top for five whole minutes. We could look down and see the lights along the shore and smell the carmel corn and cotton candy and hear the music and the people. . . .

And I thought of Lilith.

I wondered if she'd made arrangements for the delivery of her new screens. She had ordered them the week before. And I worried if Mr. Cummings was letting Lord Jim roam the neighborhood or if he had him tied up.

One night I woke up in the middle of the night, and I could hear rain on the cabin roof. No one else was awake, and it was just me and the rain and the dark. I snuggled down under the covers and got to thinking about the days with Lilith. They were not really so bad. Of course, there had been the so-so days. Lilith called them the "oatmeal days," but there had been fun days too.

The rest of the week I kept thinking about Lilith. I didn't love her, that was for sure. But I liked her. There was a difference. Some people you loved; some people you liked. The people you loved, you thought about when they weren't around. The people you liked you never thought of until they just happened along.

But I still kept thinking about Lilith, even though I didn't send her a postcard.

THE NURSING HOME

"WE'RE GOING OUT to call on Mattie McDonald today."

I washed down the bite of cookie with the last of my milk, rinsing the coldness around in my mouth.

We'd started having a midmorning snack on the back porch since we came back from our vacations.

"It's nice to stop in the middle of busyness and just sit." Lilith explained. "Just sit and shake out the dust."

"Shake out the dust?"

"The dust of the mind."

Lilith still talked funny sometimes.

"Where does Mattie live?"

"In the Home."

"The nursing home?"

"Yes. The nursing home."

IT LOOKED LIKE A SCHOOL, a stack of yellow bricks in a fringe of dull green junipers.

Twilight Meadows, the sign said.

Lilith walked slower than usual, but I wished she'd slow down even more and delay opening the glass doors, which looked black from the reflection of the trees.

"Why do they call it Twilight Meadows?"

"Why? Because some people think in metaphors. Twilight is the time between sunset and dark."

"Oh."

We were almost to the black doors.

"There isn't much meadow, though."

Lilith chuckled, her throat jiggling, her lips tight.

"No. Not much meadow."

"They could call it what it really is. A place for old people to live."

Lilith paused before the black doors, shifted the sack of cookies she was taking to Mattie and looked down at me.

"Do you know, I believe you have the clearest blue eyes I've ever seen. Your grandmother Pearl had eyes like that."

The hall, too, was like a school with doors opening off and even a principal's office with a receptionist.

"May I help you?" Her voice dipped down and up with sweetness.

"We came to see Mattie McDonald. She's out of the infirmary now, I believe."

The woman pulled open a long drawer.

"McDonald. McDonald. I'll check this other file. Can't always keep track of room assignments. High turnover, you know."

Lilith nodded, smiling only with her lips.

It was like a school with steel files and important-looking papers on big desks, and on the wall a bright blue poster with red letters: *Everyone smiles at Twilight Meadows.*

The smell was different from school, though: musty, sour, stale with medicine, coffee, and soap.

"Mattie McDonald's been put in 136 West."

It was a strange word, *put.*

I touched Lilith's arm as we moved down the long hall of doors.

"What's that funny smell?"

Our footsteps echoed against the walls.

"It's the smell of sadness. You've probably never smelled it before."

"I don't like it. It stinks funny."

"It does just that. It stinks funny."

A small man hobbled toward us, his hair waving like dust webs in a breeze.

"Good afternoon, Mr. Kelly."

"She's got the soul of a gopher and the neck of a swan," sang Mr. Kelly.

I moved closer to Lilith.

"He's all right. Mr. Kelly thinks in metaphors too."

A frail gray wisp of a creature drooped over the arm of her wheelchair.

"How are you, Mrs. Shelby?"

"I'm old."

She did not lift her eyes as we walked past.

"What did you mean, metaphors?"

Lilith was peering up at the brass numbers on the doors.

"It's calling something what it isn't."

"That's lying."

"More like hiding dust, instead of shaking it out. This place is a convenient rug for some families."

"The home is like a hotel, though, isn't it? Or maybe a motel—except everybody's so old. I mean . . . well, it's sort of nice. Some of the rooms. Pretty rugs and nice furniture."

"Oh, *things* are new enough. That's not what's wrong. It's that the people got old. Outstayed their welcome. A good guest knows when to leave. But not all guests. That's it, isn't it? 136 West. Check it for me, will you?"

"136 West."

Mattie McDonald lay propped up in the hospital bed, arms like yellowing twigs against the white sheet, eyes focused on a TV set.

"We'll wait," Lilith whispered. "Mattie always watches 'As the World Turns' and 'General Hospital.' It will be over soon."

"Soap operas?"

"When you can no longer feel, it's nice to have something feel for you. And Mattie has the best color TV in Twilight Meadows."

Lilith slipped into the blue plastic arm chair inside the door, her red dress shimmering with her breathing. I stood behind, my arm resting along the back of the chair. I looked down on Lilith's head, the hair parting like strands of silk, the scalp clean and pink. I wondered what it would feel like to lay my hand on the soft whiteness.

Over the life-like voices from the TV, now engaged in a frightening argument, came a low, soft crooning like a lone owl in a forest: "Coo. Coo. Coooooo."

It was coming from behind a curtain that divided the small room.

Lilith moved her head and spoke from the corner of her mouth.

"It's little Bertha. She only coos."

"Doesn't she know she's doing it?"

"Do you always know you're biting your nails?"

"But she's making noise."

Lilith did not answer.

The music from the TV swelled and blanketed the actors' final words. The episode was over. With fumbling fingers,

Mattie clicked off the remote control.

Lilith pushed herself up from the chair and moved to the bed.

"Mattie?" Her voice was soothing. "I'm so glad to see you're out of the infirmary."

Mattie turned her head slowly to look at Lilith, her eyes clouded as if trying to sort out the unreal Lilith from the real of the soap operas.

"Lilith?" Her voice sounded like an apology.

"It's Lilith, Mattie. And I brought you three of my finest Super-Simple-Chocolate-Covered-Peanut-Clusters. You can suck on the peanuts. And keep them hidden. You're not supposed to have them."

With both hands, Mattie crumpled the sack and slipped it under the bed sheets.

"And you've got on a new gown, Mattie. How pretty."

Mattie looked down and fingered the pink lace on the collar.

"Thorben brought it to me."

"How nice!" Lilith took the tiny hands in her own.

"Thorben comes to see me every day."

"Of course he does, Mattie. Thorben loves you."

"Hasn't missed a day, Lilith."

"I know. I know, Mattie, dear."

Mattie looked over at me with dull eyes. "Who's that?"

"This is Ellen. My Ellen. My companion. I'm home now, you know. Ellen takes care of me and I take care of her. We take care of each other."

Lilith didn't often call me Ellen, but never had she called me "My Ellen."

Lilith turned and muttered to me, "Thorben's been dead for thirty-five years. She'll remember in a few minutes."

"The days are so long, Lilith. And time means nothing. When will Thorben come?"

I moved back to the plastic chair.

"Is that a car, Lilith? Do you hear it in the drive? Thorben's coming today ... to take me home ... he promised. .... He's coming today."

Lilith rested one elbow on the bed, her fingers cupped like a shell over her brow. What a big woman Lilith Adams was. I had never realized it before: broad face topped by white hair, faintly streaked with amber and brushed upward from the wide forehead, and muscles running up the sides of her neck from strong shoulders.

"I've decided to wear my green knit, Lilith, when Thorben comes for me ... when Thorben comes. He should be here by now ... he's never late."

"Coo. Coo. Cooooooo" came the voice from behind the curtain.

WE DID NOT STAY LONG at Twilight Meadows.

I'm sure Lilith would have stayed longer, but a woman in a white uniform rolled in a wheelchair with a loud, "Well, Mattie, how are *we* today?"

There was hardly enough of Mattie to make an "I," let alone a "we."

"Mattie goes down to the dining room now for her tea. Don't we, Mattie?" shouted the nurse while the voice behind the curtain cooed on like a tired mourning dove.

I wondered if she thought Mattie was deaf. If so, Lilith hadn't realized it, for she had been answering Mattie in comforting murmurs, so low, I could hardly hear.

"But I haven't had my breakfast yet."

"Now, Mattie. We had breakfast. Remember? Oatmeal? And toast?"

"Breakfast?"

"And we had our lunch too. Cottage cheese. Beef soup. And now it's time for our tea."

"Tea?" Mattie repeated as the nurse lifted her into the wheelchair, the new gown with the pink lace falling away from limp legs the color of old snow.

"I'll come out again to see you, Mattie dear." Lilith bent over the wheelchair and touched the drooping cheek with her fingertips.

"Tea?"

"Coo. Coo. Coooooo" agreed the mourning dove behind the curtain.

Tea at Twilight Meadows had the same effect as "Recess" at Moore Elementary School. Doors opened. Halls filled. Except it was all in slow motion: the feet "swish . . . put, swish . . . put, swish . . . put" down the dull tile floor. And a terrible waiting, not like the waiting for a recess bell, but just waiting.

"It's really like a school—sort of," I said as Lilith and I followed the people down the long hall now golden from the late afternoon sun.

"I guess that's what it is, Ellen. A school for old children." Lilith turned to look at me.

One thing about Lilith I liked. Lilith listened when I talked, her eyes intent, as if I were the most important thing in the world. Of course, if she didn't agree with me, her head would tip back, her eyes still on me, as if she had grown inches taller and were looking down from a great new height.

"Yes, yes. Oh, yes. You are most right, child. It *is* a school for old children. To learn how to die. . . . No. No. To *unlearn* how to live."

"It should be nicer."

We were approaching the dining hall.

"Lots of things should be nicer. Remember that poem I read you from Browning:

Grow old along with me
The best is yet to be
The last of life
For which the first was made.

It should be like that. Nice, like sunsets. But sunsets are beautiful only if you are not the sun."

Sometimes I didn't have any trouble understanding Lilith.

WE CAME OUT of the black doors and into the afternoon sun.

"Sure smells better out here."

"Do you know what I feel like doing, Ellen?" Lilith's mouth moved up at the ends, the wrinkles like parentheses. "I feel like running clear down to the end of this walk without stopping once! Let's do! Nobody's looking."

And we did.

Except Lilith did have to stop before we reached the end of the walk.

BREAK-STEP DAY

IT'S A BREAK-STEP DAY."

Lilith had the wicker basket out on the kitchen table and was pulling napkins from a box on the counter.

"Break-Step Day?"

"Yes. Break-Step. A Break-Step Day is hanging out your wash at four in the afternoon when the whole neighborhood has had theirs out since eight in the morning. It's sleeping until noon or getting up at four in the morning to see the sun rise. A Break-Step Day, Ellen, is doing what you want to do, when you want to do it."

'You mean it? What do we want to do?"

"We'll pack a lunch and paddle up the inlet. We can take Mr. Cummings's canoe. He drove down to the lake early this morning and got it out of his boat house. It's tied up at the public dock all ready for us."

"Can we stay all day?"

"We certainly can. And we'll let the current carry us home. We'll all like that."

"All? Who's all?"

"Grace, of course. She'll come. At least, I hope so. When you scoot up and invite her. Be good for her. Get her out into the air. Breathe some sunshine for a change. Run tell her now."

Lilith moved toward the refrigerator. "Tell her she'd best bring her thermos. And mind, close the screen door behind you."

I slammed it shut with my elbow and headed toward Grace's house. I couldn't see why we had to drag her along. One old woman was enough. Not that Lilith was that bad. She really wasn't, and she didn't always seem seventy-seven years old.

The morning was quiet except for an occasional slam of a screen door and the burring of locusts hidden high in the trees. As I walked up the street, drifts of dust puffed up from beneath my bare feet. Drops of sweat formed between my shoulder blades and trickled down my back. It would be cooler on the lake, and in the inlet the trees would filter the sun.

Grace's front yard was like Lilith's needle point hanging above the living room sofa. Flowers edged the walk. The colors, the scents, even the sizes of the blossoms were perfect. Lilith's garden looked as if someone had taken handfuls of seeds and tossed them up, and they grew wherever they landed.

Grace's front porch was shady and cool as I lifted the brass knocker and heard it echoing inside the house.

"Oh, my dear. You look so warm. Come in where it's cool. And have some lemonade. I was just getting ready to sit down and have a glass myself."

Grace moved down the hallway, her arms stretched out as if she were swimming, and I, a minnow, following in her wake.

"I'm supposed to ask you if you'd like to go for a canoe ride up the inlet. With Lilith and me."

Grace handed me a glass of lemonade and floated over to an ancient wing-backed chair beside the fireplace. She could have been my age, she was so small—if I didn't look at her face and hands.

"A canoe trip? Oh, dear. I don't know. I don't swim very well."

"But we'll be in the canoe. And there's life preservers. And I can swim real good."

"Oh, the egotism of youth! I'm sure you can, Little Dolly. And I know Lilith is most capable. Why, when we were girls in school, we used to have regattas on the lake and Lilith always won the canoeing event."

"Oh?"

I hoped it wasn't going to be another afternoon of when-I-was-a-girl.

"And Lilith said to bring your thermos."

I wasn't sure Grace heard me. I didn't repeat it.

MR. CUMMINGS DROVE US ALL down to the public dock. Lilith had trouble getting into his old Mercury. She could get everything in except her right foot.

"After that tumble down the cellar stairs, it doesn't always do what I want it to do."

So after Mr. Cummings had helped Grace into the back seat with me, he walked around the car, gently lifted Lilith's right ankle, and placed her foot carefully in on the floor mat. "Is that comfortable now, Lil?"

"Fine. Just fine. It's a funny thing, Mr. Cummings. That leg never bothers me except sometimes when I try to climb into your car."

I had noticed that too.

At the lake, Mr. Cummings and I pulled the canoe up on the sandy beach and held it steady until Grace and Lilith were seated. We pushed and shoved, and as I leaped in, the canoe hit the water and we were off.

"Now take care, Lil. Stay in where the water's shallow."

"Of course. Of course. Now you're not to worry, Mr. Cummings. I was raised on this lake. I know every ripple and turn."

"I'll be back to pick you up around three."

We paddled along close in to shore, and when we moved under the stone bridge, the quiet closed in upon us. We were in a bayou, a back water really, with a small island in the center, heavy with stunted underbrush. Lilith sat in the stern switching her paddle from side to side. She guided us far to the right of the island and down into the blue-green inlet.

At our approach, herons nesting in the tall elms and birches took off, their huge wings fanning the air. A lone mud hen made a perfect V in the water ahead.

Grace sat in the bow, her back fragile. Through her sheer blouse, her shoulder blades pushed like little fishbones as she sipped from her thermos cup.

"It's a whole different world, isn't it, Grace?"

"Like moving back in time . . . like when we were girls together, Lilith, and everything was possible."

"We'll keep going a little farther. We can beach the canoe on Cottonwood Point and have our lunch. Be on the lookout for deer."

I sat cross-legged in the middle of the canoe, dipping my paddle lazily into the green-brown water. Tree leaves rustled on the bank. A killdeer called from the depths of the woods. No one spoke.

I looked down at my hands, dappled by shadows, and they seemed drawn and wrinkled like Lilith's. I leaned over the edge of the canoe and looked into the water. The ripples distorted my face into wrinkles and I imagined my hair streaming out, thin and white. Would I grow old too?

I shuddered and matched Lilith's rhythmic strokes.

"Lilith, dear. Do you see those birds ahead?" Grace asked.

"I see them. Why? Are they a strange species?"

I squinted past Grace's shoulder.

"No. No, I don't think so. But, Lilith . . . they appear . . . oh, my dear, they *do* appear to be walking on water."

Lilith pulled her paddle out and rested it across the gunwale of the canoe.

"Nonsense, Grace. A trick of light. The channel runs true and deep through here. Paddle on."

Except Grace had yet to pick up her paddle.

"I say, Lilith. Look again. Those birds ahead. They *are* walking on water."

My paddle was pulled from my hand. I grabbed, but there was no need. The paddle did not disappear. It stuck like a flagpole in the water. The canoe was not moving.

"Well, we seem to have lost the channel," Lilith chuckled and examined the mud clinging to the length of her own paddle.

Grace turned her head, and I noticed for the first time the fine blue veins that lay close under the clear white skin of her temple.

"Whatever shall we do?" cried Grace. "Perhaps one of us should get out and turn the canoe around."

I was already half out of the canoe. "I'll do it. I can pull."

The mud was soft and warm against my legs.

Grace sipped again from her cup and patted her lips with a lace-edged handkerchief. "Do be careful where you step, child. There are probably all sorts of creatures in there." She peered over the bow into the two inches of water that covered the mud flat.

"Pole. Don't talk. Pole and help the child." Lilith sat in the stern, her feet firmly braced. "All together now. Pole!"

Fifteen minutes later, Lilith and I pulled and poled the canoe to shore with Grace, like a delicate river queen in the bow, directing. "There. Just there. No, a little to the right. There."

We were beached on a grassy mound with sumac and willows drooping over the water.

"What a lovely spot. Oh, Lilith. I do believe I see a patch of gentians." Grace lay down, flat on her back, in the long grass. "You two sit down and rest too. It's so lovely here. Like your song, Lilith. What is it now? 'The gentians fringed with . . . with glue.' "

"Blue, Grace. Blue."

And for the first time that summer, Lilith looked down at me and winked. I winked back.

Lilith propped her back against a tree and stretched her legs. A wood ant crawled up her sturdy shoe and across her leg. The ankle was trim and neat, and I marveled how ankles didn't get old like faces. At least they didn't look old.

I lay back in the grass and watched the clouds turning and twisting and flowing into shapes: old men trailing wisps of beards, witches with white streaming hair, dragons with curling tails. I saw Lilith's face in the clouds and Grace's and even my own. Then they all ran together in a feathery billow that turned into a ship.

We didn't wake Grace for lunch.

"The sleep will do her more good than lunch."

Lilith and I ate the cold chicken and potato salad with the thick slabs of homemade bread, and we talked about watersnakes and dragon flies and catfish and frogs and toadstools and arrowhead plants, their snowy white flowers jutting out of the water like Easter lilies.

"The Sioux called them swamp potatoes. The women would wade into these very swamps and harvest the roots by breaking them off with their toes."

I waded out and picked some leaves, each one shaped like an arrowhead. I arranged them on the bank in a circle, the ends of the leaves pointing into the center. Lilith said it looked like a sign of the zodiac.

"Quite artistic, really."

Lilith named all the trees on the bank—water birch, swamp willow, basswood, slippery elm. The bushes—sumac, wild gooseberry, elderberry. And the flowers—shoestrings, sheepshowers hidden deep in the grass, wild violets, and even a bloodroot that bled real blood when I snipped off a leaf.

We didn't have to paddle going back; the current from the inlet carried us down past the island and under the stone bridge. We followed a muskrat that dipped and swam and left a shimmering trail in the water until he disappeared completely. Lilith spotted him again, climbing up the opposite bank far ahead.

Mr. Cummings was waiting for us at the dock.

"Began to think you might have had trouble."

"No trouble at all, Mr. Cummings," called Grace, who had dozed most of the ride back until we saw the muskrat.

"No trouble, Mr. Cummings," echoed Lilith.

"And what a marvelous afternoon we had," Grace piped as Mr. Cummings held her hand as she stepped from the canoe.

"But she slept most of the time, Lilith," I whispered.

"Never mind," Lilith answered as she swung her paddle over her shoulder like a rifle. "Grace needs a lot of rest."

"But we did all the paddling."

"I know. Some of us paddle. Some of us ride."

Mr. Cummings dropped me off at my house first. Skeet Barclay was shooting baskets out in the drive. I snatched the ball as it came bouncing down across the walk and drove in for a quick lay-up.

"Where you and the Gray Panthers been?"

"We took Mr. Cummings's canoe and went up the inlet. You ever been there in a canoe?"

"Been there in the winter. Skated down there once. Never in the summer." He arched a one-hander over my head. "Suppose old Cummings would loan us his canoe some day? If you asked him?"

"Maybe. I could ask. We saw herons and muskrats and all sorts of things. We had fun. Picnic too. Chicken."

But I didn't tell Skeet about Lilith's getting the canoe stuck in the mud. I knew he would really crack up over it, but somehow I didn't want him to laugh at Lilith.

BOOK-AND-BASKET

BOOK-AND-BASKET MET the last Friday of every month, except when it had to be postponed because of Easter, Thanksgiving, Christmas, Fourth of July, Memorial Day, and February.

"Can't depend on the weather in February."

"Sounds as if you postpone it more than you meet."

"It does, doesn't it? *Book* means one of us reviews a book. And *basket* . . . well, now what do *you* think it means?"

"Bring your own lunch?"

"That's youth for you. Minds in their stomachs. The body's so important . . . when you're young." Lilith paused. "No, Ellen, we each bring a basket for our fancy work. Our knitting, embroidery, crocheting."

"Oh."

At least Lilith hadn't made me learn how to knit or crochet.

"I'm a charter member. Only two of us left. Grace and I. Grace usually forgets, though. The club was near extinction at one time. Split down the middle over whether we should serve a full lunch or dessert."

"I know whose side I'd be on."

"The problem was," Lilith hastened to explain, "it would mean changing the meeting time. Now who wants dessert in the middle of the afternoon?"

"Who won?"

"The Lunchers won. By one vote. Grace remembered to come that day."

"Grace remembered!"

"Oh, Maybelle was furious. She was for dessert. Accused me of manipulating the vote by reminding Grace. But it was no such thing. I just happened to stop in at Grace's that day."

"Now, Lilith," I said.

"Well, it's a fact. She was a little under the weather, and I thought Book-and-Basket would cheer her up."

"I believe you."

"I've always thought," Lilith chuckled, "a better name might have been Book-Basket-and-*Bread*."

"Now you're telling the truth."

Lilith rapped me on the seat with a spatula.

I decided, as I got "cleaned up" for the meeting that the order was still wrong. It should have been Bread first, for the book part usually lasted ten minutes, with the rest of the two hours for lunch.

Usually I sat out under the willow during Lilith's club meetings, but that Friday the sky was overcast and the air, muggy. An early morning shower had left water standing on the lawns.

"Get out *Macbeth*. You can read a scene or two and then later you can help with the lunch."

We had been reading *Macbeth* that week in our four-to-five hour.

But it was the *Book* that took over the *Basket* and *Bread* that Friday. Grace reviewed the latest best seller.

At first there were polite little gasps as Grace announced the title, but as she fluttered on, the gasps grew to mutters and shocked side glances in Lilith's direction.

"Stop her, Lilith!" whispered Maybelle. "Think of the child. It's so descriptive!"

"Never mind," Lilith whispered back. "Grace hasn't told us anything we don't already know. It's the truth, isn't it? It's natural."

"It may be, but do we have to talk about it?"

"I don't think it hurts at all to talk about it."

Grace, hearing the mutterings, looked up from her page. Lilith smiled back, and Grace continued.

There was a tight-lipped silence when Grace completed her "review." Maybelle cleared her throat. Grace looked around the circle, but nobody clapped.

"What a *fine* review, Grace dear," came Lilith's sweetest voice, slithering through the silence. "And what an interesting approach. Where *did* you find such a book?"

"In the library. It's new." Grace smoothed her dress over her knees with shaking fingers, her eyes on the floor.

"But, Lilith. . . ." began Maybelle. "Really, I. . . ."

"I tell you, I'm going right down and check it out for myself the minute Grace returns it. Such lovely imagery. What was it Martha said there at the last—'Life consists of birth and love and death, all rolled up in a multicolored ball for bouncing.' That is lovely, isn't it, Maybelle? Life, a multicolored ball for bouncing."

There were soft sputterings from the Book-and-Baskets. I was glad Lilith was sticking up for Grace and not getting embarrassed like everyone else.

Lilith edged her chair over beside Grace's rocker, and Grace, like a wilting flower moved into the sun, sat taller as Lilith continued, "Did the rain ruin your iris, Grace dear?"

By the time lunch arrived, served on the best dinner plates, the book was forgotten.

I sat on an uncomfortable chair in the far corner amid the bubble of voices and the soft scrapings of silver salad forks on china. "A multicolored ball for bouncing." I drew the ball in my mind: red, white, and blue splashes over a shiny plastic globe. I tossed the ball into the air and it bounced back. I was going to toss it even higher, but Lilith interrupted with, "Ellen. More coffee for Maybelle, please."

The battle of the book, however, was not over. The next day the *Book* bounced back.

"Ellen. Run down to the library and check out that book Grace reviewed yesterday. Put it on my card."

I returned without the book.

"Did you get it?"

"It . . . it wasn't there. I looked."

"Didn't you ask?"

"I asked. It wasn't there. Maybe Grace hasn't taken it back."

"Oh, I'm sure she has. She was going to drop it off on her way home yesterday."

I didn't want to tell Lilith the truth because I didn't want to disappoint her. I tried to sidestep the question.

"Are you sure? Did you ask at the main desk?"

"I asked."

I sampled one of Lilith's freshly baked cookies.

"El-len!" Lilith's voice dipped down and up.

Lilith was not a sidestepper. Lilith waded through.

"Mr. Forsling said . . . he said. . . ."

"What *did* he say, Ellen?"

"He said it wasn't there."

"What do you mean wasn't there?"

"He said it had been . . . removed. Removed from the shelf. That's what he said. Exactly."

"Removed from the shelf!" Lilith spun around.

"For reconcentration or something like that."

"Could you mean reconsideration?"

I nodded.

Lilith was shouting. I was sure Mr. Cummings would hear her and come running.

"How could they do such a thing?"

"Who's they?"

"Can't you see? Someone . . . someone in Book-and-Basket complained. Complained to Mr. Forsling about the book. And he'd have to take it off the shelf until the Library Board looked at it."

"Who? Who complained?"

"Someone in Book-and-Basket. Who would do such a thing to Grace? Or to me?"

"Maybelle, I bet."

"Maybelle? Oh, never Maybelle."

I wasn't so sure. Once I had heard Maybelle say, "Lilith collects friends like stray cats." And Grace had snapped back, "Well, it's something neither you nor I ever learned to do, Maybelle," and her hands shook so badly she spilled her drink down the front of her dress.

"I suppose it doesn't matter who. It's the principle. The principle of freedom of choice. No one has the right to censor *my* reading."

"What are you going to do?"

"I'm going to register my complaint. I'll go to the next Library Board meeting. Why, the book might be a classic some day. Why do some people see only evil? Evil lies in the eyes of the beholder. The sad part is the good has to rely on the beholder too."

I was all tangled up in Lilith's words.

LIKE MOLLY PITCHER with her loaded cannon, Lilith strode up the steps that Wednesday to register her complaint with the Library Board. I went along.

"You needn't go in. Sit here in the hall and watch my purse. This should take only a minute."

"Do you think you'll get the book?"

"It isn't just the book, Ellen. It's the principle. Odds are always against you when you try to change something, but trying is what it's all about. Never forget that."

I didn't dare forget, if Lilith told me to remember.

I sat in the empty hall on a bench, a bench with open slats for seat and back. I was not comfortable. I thought it was probably made that way so people couldn't wait for Library Board meetings.

I hoped Lilith would get her book even if she didn't get her principle. When I thought of the word "principle," the image of Miss Patrick, sitting in her office across from the sixth grade room and making rules, always took over, even though I knew it meant something else.

I wished I could do something to help Lilith.

"Please, God," I breathed, "let Lilith have her book—and her principle."

On second thought, I withdrew the principle from my prayer in the interest of not appearing too greedy.

"Just the book, God," I compromised in a half whisper and rearranged myself on the slatted bench.

The hall was empty, extending both ways like a tunnel.

Lilith's minutes were always so long. But waiting makes minutes long.

I slid off the bench and walked on tiptoe down the hall, gazing at the new books in bright covers displayed behind glass cases that reached almost to the floor.

On one cover a girl in flowing skirts was running through long grass. Behind her in the distance, a covered wagon with a heavy oxen team struggled to cross a blue river. I wondered what it would be like to be that girl.

Without an effort I *was* the girl on the book cover. I was inside the glass case. It was an easy thing to do, to move into the case. All I had to do was think it and I was there. Now I could see out into the hall and down the hall. The wind whipped my skirt against my legs. The grass smelled newly baked in the prairie heat. I could hear the clang of chains and the crack of the driver's whip from the distant wagon. My feet sank into a tangle of grass. I almost tripped.

The library door opened and shut with a sharp click. I was out of the glass case and back in the hall.

Lilith had her book cradled in the crook of her arm. I ran back to the bench and snatched up Lilith's purse.

"You got your book?"

"I got my book."

Lilith's neck was blotched with red. A lock of her hair hung loose over one ear.

"And the principle too?"

"And the principle too."

I trotted down the stone steps behind Lilith. I was glad God had been so nice to give Lilith both.

"Compromise on *things,* girl. But *never* on principle."

I nodded. The words had a nice little rhythm for easy remembering.

"I'm sure glad you won."

"Won?" Lilith snorted as she doubled her stride. "I didn't *win* it, I earned it."

I skipped up beside her.

"Can we read it today, in our four-to-five hour?"

Lilith stopped in midstride and turned, "Listen, you. You may be old for your age, but don't get it into your head that you're that old."

"But you said yourself it was good. And I thought it was

interesting, the things Grace talked about."

"You are *not* reading it. And that's final."

"But that's not fair!"

"Fair or not. That's the way it's going to be."

"I can't see what's the difference between the library not letting you read it and your not letting me read it."

Lilith did not answer right away, but by the time we started down from Farley's cottonwood, she said, in a funny tight voice, not at all like Lilith's, "It's a matter of principle."

AFRAID

THE STORM HAD HUNG in the southwest all morning, building up into black banks that kept pushing the blue skyline eastward. Gusts of wind swept in across the town sending dust twisting down the streets, followed by a sudden calm.

The two of us had rescued a reluctant Lord Jim from his clothesline post and hustled him into the kitchen. Lilith rushed to her bedroom to save the newly-laundered curtains now whipping out into the room like parade banners.

I was afraid of storms.

"Now, then," sighed Lilith. "I guess we're all battened down. We'd better go out on the porch and keep an eye out. This may turn into a twister. We should be ready to run for the cellar."

Next to storms, I was afraid of cellars, especially Lilith's cellar, even on the hottest day. It was dark and damp and smelled of unlighted places with the furnace and water heater lurking like monsters in the far corner.

My fear would begin when Lilith, peering into cupboards, searching shelves, closing doors with exasperated slams, would exclaim, "Isn't that funny. I thought I had an extra jar. Run down to the cellar and fetch me some more corn relish. It's in the far cupboard on the top shelf."

I had to force myself to go down, leaving the door open and switching on the light before I took a single step.

Finally I managed to find a safe way into Lilith's cellar by repeating my own magic formula.

The words were meaningless. I think they came from some poem Lilith read once in the four-to-five hour: "I gain the cove with pushing prow."

I would repeat the words on every step down: "I gain the cove with pushing prow." Step. "I gain the cove with pushing prow." Step. "I gain the cove with pushing prow." Step.

Going back up, I could get clear to the top on just the one line: "I . . . gain . . . the . . . cove . . . with . . . pushing . . . prow."

I needed a magic formula to go down into a cellar. For storms, I had no formula.

"ALWAYS WATCH CLOUDS in the southwest. If they are dark and stormy with a yellowish tinge and are boiling, it's a tornado. Fascinating to watch, though. A storm is a battle, you know. Between the earth and the sky. We'll sit here in the porch swing and watch."

It wasn't much of a choice: the porch or the cellar. I decided I'd stay with Lilith.

Lilith gave the porch swing a push with her foot.

"We could play a game while we wait for the storm. Let me see now. We could . . . I know. Why don't we tell each other what we're most afraid of? That could be fun, don't you think?"

"I suppose so."

I wondered if Lilith knew I was afraid.

"I'll go first. Shall I?"

"Okay."

"Well, let's see now. I'll have to think. Seventy-seven years of living takes a bit of thinking over. Well . . . when I was little, I was afraid of the dark. Even if the stars were out and the moon too, I was still afraid of the dark, of being alone in the dark. It was silly, of course, wasn't it?"

"I suppose."

"But once, once my brother and I were sent to close the gate down in the far pasture. It was dark. In June, I remember. After we'd closed the gate and climbed back up Lyons Hill, we both lay down in the grass, on our backs, to rest. And Barney—he was my brother—Barney started pointing out the stars. The Big Dipper, the Seven Sisters, the Milky Way, the North Star. And he said he liked the dark even better than day. He said it was like velvet.

"Then I told him I was afraid of the dark. I think he knew that. 'What's to be scared of?' he asked me, and I said the dark was so much of nothing and that's what made it scary."

"I don't like the dark either."

"But do you know, Ellen, from that time on I learned to look for the stars instead of thinking of the dark. I know the stars well now."

"Where's your brother?"

"Barney?"

"Yeah."

"He was older than I. He's gone."

Rain, driven by sharp surges of the wind, beat against the porch windows.

"It's your turn. What are you afraid of?"

At first I didn't want to tell Lilith what I was afraid of. I felt as if I were opening forbidden doors.

"Sometimes . . . I'm afraid of big buildings. Like a different school or a big office building."

"Is it the bigness?" Lilith asked seriously.

"I don't know. It makes me feel small. That's when I get scared."

"I suppose it's sort of like the dark—the nothingness. Makes us all feel small. But a big building is just a bunch of little buildings stuck together."

"I never thought of it that way."

"We all feel small sometime or other. But we do have a balloon inside. And when you feel small, try taking a deep breath and blowing up that balloon. Try that the next time you're in a big building . . . or around anything that makes you feel small. Usually takes several breaths, though, to blow it up, but you'll be surprised how much breath you can find for blowing when you have to."

I gulped in a sharp breath as lightning forked out over the roof of Mr. Cummings's house.

"It's my turn again. Let me see. What else frightens me? Would you believe. . . ."

Lilith was a pauser. She always paused before she said something that you knew was going to be especially important or exciting.

"Would you believe I used to be afraid of storms?"

"Storms?"

"Oh, my, yes. When I was little—five or six maybe—I used to throw a tantrum like you've never seen. I'd stand by the window and scream and shake and shiver and carry on. But one night, when we were having a terrible storm, my father swooped me up, perched me on his shoulder, covered me with his old windbreaker, and toted me right out into the middle of that storm."

"That's awful!"

"No. No. Indeed not. He showed me the storm. Told me all about it. How the lightning was a big electric spark. That if you counted between the flash and the thunder—one-Mississippi, two-Mississippi, three-Mississippi—you knew how far away it was. How lightning purified the air. And how thunder sounded like trucks rolling over a wooden bridge."

"It does sound like that."

"And I've loved storms ever since. Just loved them."

"You have?"

"Indeed I have. Now it's your turn again."

I squirmed farther back into the porch swing.

"This is going to sound awful dumb. But sometimes I'm afraid of faces."

"People-faces?"

"Uh huh. Not all faces. Grown-up faces mostly. Not the people. Just the faces."

"My face too?"

I giggled.

"Not yours."

"What about faces scares you? The mouths? The noses?"

I shook my head.

"I guess it's just that I never know where to look when people look at me."

Lilith sucked in a big breath. It sounded as if she were filling her own balloon.

"You should try looking into eyes. Eyes are the nicest part of a face. Mouths you can't depend on. Noses are so fixed, and chins, nobody can help chins. But eyes. Eyes are the real person looking out."

Through the rain-washed windows, Mr. Cummings's pine looked like a finger painting, smudged and distorted into a blob of dripping green.

We sat in silence except for the rhythmic creak of the porch swing, but we were both used to the silences now. "Talking without words," Lilith called it.

The wind dropped and the rain settled down to a soft patter.

"I don't suppose anything frightens you any more," I said.

Lilith stopped the swing with her foot. She didn't answer right away. Then in a voice I hardly recognized, she said, "I'm no braver than you, Ellen. Maybe not as brave. You go out under the willow—all alone—and I watch from the kitchen window and envy you. I'm afraid of being alone. Not *being* alone as much as being *left* alone. Of being of no use to anyone. Of not being needed. Only needing. Needing to take, and not being able to give. For what I have to give, no one wants . . . anymore."

"I've never been afraid of that."

"I'm afraid of the way I feel, some days, unless I talk myself out of it. Of being outdated. Of not being old enough to be a genuine antique. Just old enough to be junk. Pure junk. And when someone asks me how old I am, I feel as if I've done something wrong by living so long. As if I had some terrible disease."

I wanted to say many things, but I didn't know how.

"I think," I began. "I think when I grow old . . . I mean grow up . . . I want to be just like you, Lilith. I think you're very brave and I don't think you're so old . . . or useless . . . or junky."

"I said *junk*. Not *junky*." It was the old Lilith back again. "This rain reminds me, I haven't watered the plants in the living room."

I really wasn't in a big hurry that day to go home. I sat cross-legged on the kitchen stool trying to sort out many things.

"Ellen. Come in here. Just see."

I hopped down from the stool.

"See what my geranium has done. Given me two new blossoms, and I haven't paid a bit of attention to her all week."

Lilith talked to her plants. She even had names for some of them.

"They hear. They understand."

"Oh, Lilith."

"You don't believe me?"

"Not really."

"Can you prove they don't hear?"

"No."

"So there. If they can't hear us, all we've wasted is a little consideration. If they can hear us, think how much joy we've given them." It was Lilith Logic. I couldn't disprove it, so I had to accept it.

"Geraniums are such nice plants. They take so little tending. Some plants you have to baby along and they still grow up puny. Geraniums are like good friends. They don't demand. They understand."

"Who?"

"Who what?"

"Who understands?"

"Geraniums, Ellen. Geraniums."

"Oh, I thought you were talking about friends."

"I was. Oh, never mind."

The rain was over, and the sun was breaking through the late afternoon sky.

"It helps, doesn't it?" I turned back as I started out the door. "It helps to talk about things, doesn't it?"

Lilith nodded.

I paused again outside the screen door.

"And we never run out of things to say, do we?"

Lilith smiled a funny smile that made her face look old and sad—almost as old as Mr. Cummings and nearly as sad as Grace.

WINTER/SUMMER

I LET THE DOOR SLAM. I didn't mean to annoy Lilith; I just forgot. She looked up from her paper.

"Yes?"

"A car's driving in. Some lady."

Lilith peered through the bay window. "Oh. It's Gertrude. Wonder why she's here. Never comes without a reason."

"Who's Gertrude?"

"My niece. Just think, an only niece and it has to be a Gertrude. Probably driving through and thought she'd check up on me. Maybe that's what relatives think they're for."

"I'll read." I hated smiling and being polite to people I didn't know, and I was afraid Lilith might insist.

"Good. She won't stay long. Never does. I'll keep her out on the porch. Whenever she comes inside, she straightens my curtains and moves my furniture around. A great one for order." She sighed and folded the newspaper. "But, I guess that's just her way."

I retreated to the swivel rocker as the porch door opened.

"Why, Gertrude. I didn't expect to see you." The wicker porch chairs creaked as they sat down.

At first I didn't bother to listen. Their words mingled with the sparrow sounds from the shrubs outside the porch. But then Lilith's voice changed.

"I'm just fine, Gertrude. Can't you see? I'm perfectly capable of taking care of myself no matter what you and Eunice think."

I peeked around the corner of the doorway. Gertrude was pacing back and forth; she was a tall woman in a soft green suit.

"But, Aunt Lilith, you're seventy-seven. You can't keep on living here like this. Winter is coming. And Twilight Meadows is a lovely place."

"I don't need a 'lovely' place. I need a *loving* place. And that's what I have right here, with my friends around, like my good neighbor, Mr. Cummings."

Gertrude sat down with a thump and I wondered for a moment if the chair would hold.

"Loving? If you mean Mr. Cummings. . . ."

"That is not what I meant at all. But now that you mention it, Gertrude, Mr. Cummings is one of my loving friends."

"Aunt Lilith! You're certainly not thinking of. . . . You wouldn't really think of marrying, would you? I mean, your house and all. And he has children of his own."

"Even Eskimos get cold feet, sleeping alone."

"Aunt Lilith!"

Mr. Cummings had children? I guess I thought he'd always been old. But I couldn't quite see what that had to do with cold feet.

"Oh, Auntie. Think of what people would say. Why, it's . . . it's silly. Perfectly silly." Gertrude's face was getting red. So was Lilith's.

"What do you think happens when you get old? Do you think you stop living? The well may look dry, but the pump still pumps." Now Lilith was walking up and down.

"Aunt Lilith, be realistic. You always said life was real. That's the one thing I remember from my summers with you."

"Sure, it's real, but you'd remove all the unpleasantness. Twilight Meadows. Golden Age. Senior Citizen. Pass Away. It is a nursing home. It is old age. And death."

"Well, let's forget that . . . and Mr. Cummings. But, Aunt Lilith, you're seventy-seven years old. What will people think of us, letting you live here by yourself? What if something happened? You don't know how that worries Eunice."

"Something always happens. That's life, Gertrude. That's why it's worth living."

"Oh, Auntie." When Gertrude said "Auntie" it didn't sound the way the word should.

"You've been talking me over with Eunice, haven't you? What would I do at Twilight Meadows, Gertrude? I wouldn't know where to look, except back. I'm not going to waste the rest of my time reliving what's behind me. I want to die here in my own home. At 212 Lake Street."

The argument continued, building up to an exasperated "Auntie."

My stomach felt queasy. Arguments did that to me. I headed for Lilith's bedroom to get away from the voices. I wished Gertrude would leave.

I sat in front of Lilith's mirror and looked into my own eyes until the voices were a soft hum. It's frightening to look at yourself that way.

"That's you," I said to the eyes. "That's where *you* live." I searched for signs of the selves Lilith had said I contained.

"All of us are many people: the people we once were, the people who have loved us, even the people who have hurt us. We're pack rats. We store away bits and pieces and somehow they turn into selves that become an *I*."

Now I stared at the mirrored image and searched for those selves. I could find only Ellen. I glanced at the faces in the faded photographs that rimmed the mirror. Their eyes stared back too.

Eyes were worse than voices. I ran from the room, through the living room and out to the porch. I stopped beside Lilith.

Gertrude looked up, startled. "Well! Who's this?"

"Mabel Groves's girl. Ellen. Pearl's granddaughter. You remember Pearl, don't you?"

"Oh, of course. She looks a little like Mabel, doesn't she? Is she visiting?"

"She visits every day. We've been together all summer."

I could feel the words pushing themselves out of my mouth and even if Skeet had been there, I couldn't have stopped them.

"Lilith takes care of me."

Lilith coughed as if she were choking. I didn't look at her.

Gertrude eyed me and turned to Lilith, "Has she been listening to all this?"

I moved closer to Lilith. Being close made me feel bigger and stronger . . . and braver.

"Ellen was reading, weren't you, Ellen? When she's reading she hears only what she reads."

It was a typical Lilith statement, but I didn't know whether I had been complimented or scolded.

Gertrude could not stay. She had "to make" a noon luncheon. She had to preside. It sounded very important.

She kissed Lilith on the cheek. She rushed out the door and the black car rolled out of the drive.

Lilith took off her glasses and wiped them against her dress. She looked past me. "I tell you. . . ."

"What?"

"What what?"

Sometimes Lilith got so busy thinking she forgot she wasn't talking.

"You were going to tell me something."

"Oh, yes. I was going to say that together we're quite formidable. It does take two. A Sherlock Holmes needs a Dr. Watson."

"She wanted you to move! To that home. You'd have to leave Lord Jim. And Mr. Cummings . . . and me!"

"That's what living is—leaving. I tell you, never become so attached to anything, nor to anyone, that you can't leave when the time comes. But you will learn that. Alone. It's something we never accept until we are forced to."

"But you aren't going to leave, are you?"

"Oh, no. Not yet. We always have a choice. That's the trump in the hand. I can lose or finesse. I think I'll finesse for a few more years."

It sounded like the afternoons of three-handed bridge. I was sure Lilith would win.

Then she sighed. "Oh, my dear Ellen, love is such a delicate monster."

"I don't understand."

"That's what I'm saying. It's the understanding that's so difficult. Hard for mothers and daughters." She looked at me. "For daughters and mothers."

She ran her fingers through her hair and looked away. "You don't love a butterfly, Ellen, by putting it in a fruit jar to keep. Now my Eunice, when she was little, could never understand that. 'But they're so pretty. I want to save them.' Then she'd cry when the butterfly died."

I sort of thought we were no longer talking about butter-flies.

"You can't tell people that. Someday both Eunice and

Gertrude will learn to love a little less and understand a little more."

"Will she be back? To talk about nursing homes? She said she would."

"Don't worry. Not right away. In the winter, maybe."

Lord Jim was yowling at the back door. It was time for his nap on the sofa. Lord Jim believed in schedules almost as much as Lilith did.

I ran to let him in. I was glad Lilith didn't have to worry. Winter was far away from summer.

ALONE

MAYBELLE ARRIVED EARLY for the Wednesday three-handed bridge, before Lilith had the silver service set out or the coffee made. They waited in the kitchen. Ten minutes. Fifteen minutes. Then they moved into the living room. Twenty minutes. Twenty-five minutes.

"I can't understand. I didn't send Ellen to remind Grace because I saw her yesterday afternoon."

Thirty minutes. Thirty-five minutes.

"Maybe you should send Ellen. It's not like her to miss Wednesdays. Unless she thinks it's still Tuesday."

Then came the quiet hum of the limousine and the front

door burst open. Grace, teetering like a bird with a wounded wing, her face white, looked only at Lilith.

"I saw *him* again. Among my irises."

Lilith's "Now, now, Grace" hummed through the broken phrases.

"But, Lilith. I did. I saw him. In the west garden."

I wondered who *he* was and almost asked, but Lilith spoke up. "Ellen. Fix the strawberry plate with cakes."

I knew she wanted me to leave, but even in the kitchen I could hear Grace's voice weaving like a thin thread through the stillness.

"From my bedroom window. Down among my iris. Oh, Lilith, it *was* him."

"Now, Grace. Sit down. Please sit down. Maybelle, get a cup."

"Just the dry stalks left . . . in my iris bed. He was holding one . . . a dry stalk. And looking up at me."

Maybelle started to say something, but Lilith's voice cut across her words. "Grace. Grace. It's all right. You were dreaming again."

"A *dead* iris stalk, Lilith. And I ran down to Papa's study. The big bay window, you know. And he. . . ."

"Yes, yes. I know. Just a bad dream," Lilith's voice like a rocking chair.

"I ran out into the garden. In my nightdress." Her voice was shrill now. "And, Lilith . . . he was gone. But I *did* see him, Lilith. I *did.*"

I waited for Maybelle's snort. Maybelle often snorted during the bridge game or when she and Lilith were arguing about politics. The snort did not come. Instead their voices faded away as they moved out to the porch. I waited and then carried out the plate of cakes, but Lilith saw me as I walked through the door, and with a shake of her head, motioned me back.

There was no three-handed bridge that day.

I munched on a cookie and tried not to listen, but it was hard not to hear. Mostly it was Grace and Lilith with an occasional explosive, "Oh, Grace. Be sensible" from Maybelle.

Finally Maybelle strode into the kitchen and dialed a number. I wondered how she could dial so fast without getting her big fingers stuck in the holes.

"You'd better come pick up Grace. She's having one of her days."

Later Lilith called to me from the porch. "Get out that shopping bag from the front closet, Ellen. I'd better pack a few things. I must go with her."

"What do you suppose sets her off?" I heard Maybelle ask.

"She was alone all day yesterday. I checked on her, but I should have stayed."

"She never did have any backbone. You know that as well as I do, Lilith."

Lilith and Maybelle were talking as if Grace weren't there—but she was, all slumped over in the wicker chair as if she really didn't have a backbone.

Lilith took me by the shoulder and steered me out of the porch and into the living room.

"You can see, Ellen, Grace is a little under the weather today. I'm going home with her, and I'll stay the night. I'll be back tomorrow morning, before you get here. You might straighten up and then you can spend the rest of the afternoon at the pool."

That afternoon there was a whole bunch of kids at the pool and we had more fun. Skeet taught me how to do a neat racing turn in the deep end of the pool. I soon forgot all about Grace.

The next morning, Lilith's phone was ringing when I opened the back door.

"Ellen?" It was Lilith. "Grace died this morning. You must manage by yourself today."

She ignored my "Oh" that came out as if I had been swimming underwater and popped up for a gulp of air.

"Water the plants. Set the garbage out. It's garbage day. Air out the spare bedroom, and pick the string beans. Mr. Cummings will be over to check on you. You might want to finish that book we started yesterday. And watch the time. Don't linger past five."

"I won't."

And Lilith hung up.

The house was suddenly emptied of all sound. I couldn't find Lord Jim. I went out to the porch to see if Mr. Cummings were on his way over, but he was nowhere in sight. I sneaked one of Lilith's cookies and took my book down to the willow, but I couldn't get past the first chapter.

I watered Lilith's plants, set out the garbage, aired out the bedroom, picked the string beans, swept the front porch steps and both sidewalks, dusted the living and dining rooms, stacked the magazines, and it was only nine-thirty.

I looked again to see if Mr. Cummings were on his way over. He wasn't.

I took another cookie and a piece of cheese from the refrigerator. I turned on the TV, but every program had people laughing. They sounded very silly. I banged out a loud "Chop Sticks" on Lilith's piano, but once through was enough. The house was even more quiet when I quit.

I checked for Mr. Cummings again. His car was in the garage. I ate another cookie. I called up Fran, but she wasn't home. Neither was Molly. I even considered calling Skeet Barclay.

By eleven-thirty I had prepared, eaten, and cleared away lunch. I tried TV again. The book again. The pool didn't open until one and the library not until two. And where was Mr. Cummings? He was supposed to check on me.

Why didn't Lilith call? Why didn't Maybelle call for Lilith? I phoned Dad's office even though I knew he was out of town for the day. I even called home just to hear the phone ring. I called for the correct time, twice, and the Dial-a-Prayer, and still it was only twelve forty-five.

At one I didn't feel like walking clear down to the pool.

Only then did I think about Grace.

I had seen her just yesterday. She didn't look any different than she usually did. A little more excited, maybe. How could she die overnight? She wasn't any older than Lilith.

I found an apple and an orange in the back of the refrigerator and decided to eat the orange since it would take longer to peel.

I heard someone in the drive. I ran to the back door, but it was the garbage collector. My head began to ache, a dull ache as if I'd been spinning on a rope swing. Maybe I was getting sick . . . like Grace.

Mr. Cummings didn't come over until three. I set out some cookies—there weren't too many left—and a glass of milk. Lilith always fed him, so I figured I should too.

"Mighty sad. About Grace. Whole town's talking."

"They are?"

"That family was always high strung. Her old granddaddy did the same thing. I remember, I was just a kid at the time, but I remember."

"Did the same thing? You mean died?"

"Called his own raffle number. Been terrible for Lilith, I bet. Hope she can manage."

Without asking Mr. Cummings what he meant by "called his own raffle number," without asking if Grace had called her own number too, without knowing how I knew—I knew— by watching Mr. Cummings choke down the last bite of cookie. I knew what Grace had done.

The glass shook as Mr. Cummings set it down on the table and wiped off his chin with the back of his hand.

"You been getting along all right by yourself?"

"Oh, yes. I did everything Lilith told me."

"Lilith tells me you're a smart one. Sharp as a tack, she says."

I did not know what to do with such praise.

"I think Lilith's smart too," I added.

"You can bet your bottom dollar on that. Ornery, sometimes,

but all in all a fine woman. Yes, a fine woman. I'd marry her if she'd have me."

"Won't she have you?"

"It's the social security. She'd get less, and then we'd have to give up one house. She won't give up hers and I can't give up mine. But we're good neighbors. The Good Book says love your neighbor, you know."

And I knew then that Mr. Cummings did just that, and it was loving and sensible and right.

"Now if you get lonely over here," he stood up and pushed the chair back under the table, "come on over. You can help me dig onions. Onions got to hang and dry during August or they're not worth a dang."

"I won't get lonely." But it was not true. There was a difference between having to be alone in a house and choosing to be alone under a willow.

I decided to do as Lilith suggested and read the book we had started even if I had to force my way through the pages. I grabbed the apple from the refrigerator and flopped down in the swivel rocker. I heard a faint tinkle and there on the rug beside the chair was Grace's cup from yesterday. The blue bluebird cup she had painted for Lilith. It was still full. Grace had hardly tasted it.

I picked up the cup carefully—Lilith would never have forgiven me if I chipped it. It was as fragile as an egg shell. I poured the stuff into the sink, and as I watched it disappear, I knew then that Grace was gone and never again would there be any more three-handed bridge on Wednesday nor any more errands to Grace's house to tell her what day it was.

I could not spend the last hour alone. I ran out the back door and over to Mr. Cummings's, and in one hour we dug five rows of onions and hung them over the rafters in his garage to dry.

That Thursday was the loneliest day I ever lived. I knew then what Lilith meant when she said she was afraid of being *left* alone.

GENTLE GRACE

GRACE'S FUNERAL WAS HELD on Saturday. Mother didn't think I should go.

"You're too young. Funerals are so emotional. Upsetting. Barbaric really."

But I reminded her I was Lilith's companion. She looked sort of flustered and said, "Well, I guess ... maybe ... in that case you *should* go. With Lilith. If she thinks you should. If she needs you."

I had to wear a dress to the funeral. My best dress was bright red with big splashes of white zigzagging across the front.

"Oh dear," moaned Mother as she slipped the dress over the

ironing board. "This certainly isn't the thing to wear to a funeral. But it's the only dress you've got that fits you anymore. You've grown so this summer. It'll have to do."

I asked Lilith about the dress.

"It's exactly the right color. A funeral is a celebration. A celebration of life for us who are left. A celebration of having lived."

I knew perfectly well what a funeral was, but the idea of a celebration made me think of banners and flags and a parade— all for Grace, who would have loved it.

The funeral was not like that at all.

"Why are we sitting here in the back of the church?"

Lilith leaned over to whisper, "We're just friends. Relatives sit up front."

But the front pews were empty—three whole rows.

"Is this Grace's church?"

Lilith nodded with a forefinger to her lips.

I had never been in the Grace Methodist Church before. I thought it was nice that Grace could have her own church for her funeral.

I could hardly see around all the people in front of me, but when everybody stood up together, as if by a signal, I saw the bank of flowers across the altar. Grace would have loved all the flowers. There were no irises, and I was glad.

The relatives were late for the funeral. Organ music had been playing—it seemed forever—before they appeared behind *it*.

"Grace?" I whispered.

Lilith nodded.

Then she pressed her best linen handkerchief against her mouth. I had wondered when she used those handkerchiefs she kept in the little side drawer of her walnut dresser.

The organ music swelled up and down and in and out like the canoe when we came out of the inlet and hit the current. It set up a tinkling burr in the stained glass window beside us, a window with a shepherd sitting on a rock with white lambs all around.

Then everyone sat down.

It was still, but I was glad the organ music was over.

Then the minister began to talk. Not really talk, but to explain in a voice that sounded very tired. It was as if he had explained all this many, many times before but if we'd just listen once more he'd give us the answers to all the questions in the world.

Next he read a story, a story about Grace. But it was more like history—when she was born and when she died and not much in between. I wouldn't have known it was about Grace if he hadn't kept saying her name.

He stopped, and it was still again. Someone coughed. Someone sniffed. I looked up at Lilith. She did not approve of people who sniffed instead of blowing their noses. She had not noticed.

A voice began to sing. I stretched up and peeked through a gap where a man's neck swerved in from his shoulder. It was Maybelle—Maybelle in a black hat that flopped down around her ears and up in front like a pirate's hat.

Maybelle sang the same way she walked, striding through the rhythm with a big voice that overpowered the organ.

Shall we gather at the river
The beautiful, the beautiful river.

I kept thinking about our canoe trip up the inlet.

Gather at the shores of the river
That flows by the throne of God.

I thought about the cold fried chicken and the potato salad and the homemade bread we ate out on Cottonwood Point that day.

After that the minister talked again, a long, long time. He had many, many more answers—in order—with a "firstly" and a "secondly." The "finally" was a long time coming.

Maybelle sang another song, but I didn't listen. I counted all the women wearing hats in the audience. The *tiny* women, according to Lilith. I counted twenty-nine.

Then we all stood up to leave. Grace got to go first. She would have liked that, too. Everybody walked very, very slowly, but then everyone was very, very old at Grace's funeral.

Outside was a long line of cars with little blue flags attached to their antennas. They did look sort of like a parade as they moved slowly through town and up the west hill toward Oak Hill Cemetery.

"Aren't we going?"

"In the morning. We'll be alone then."

I wasn't sure which "we" Lilith meant.

We walked home through empty streets. I think everybody in town went to Grace's funeral.

"It was . . . nice," I said.

Lilith was so silent I felt as if I were walking alone. She looked down at me, the wrinkles in her forehead deepening. "Nice? I suppose."

"Is it hard to die, Lilith?"

"No. It's hard to live . . . as Grace discovered."

We sat together with Lord Jim on the back steps.

"I don't think it's hard to live. You just wake up every morning and live."

"The decisions, the choices."

"Who gets choices? I sure don't."

"Remembering, when you get old, that there *are* choices that you are still capable of making. I believe it's called 'hanging in'."

I slipped off my shoes.

"Were you ever sorry you did something, Lilith? I mean, if you could do it all over again, would you do things the same?"

"I wouldn't change the big things. I would the little. I think I'd spend more time sitting under a willow. Throw out my clocks and live on sun time. I'd slam the screen door more often, and I believe I'd kick off my shoes and go bare-footed—so I could touch growing things. I might even forget *who* and *whom*. And I would *want*—want so strongly that I could trade a summer of my life for a ten-speed bicycle.''

I stroked Lord Jim, letting his tail run through my half-closed fist. I wanted to stand right up and say, "See? I told you!" for Lilith was seeing eye-to-eye with *me*.

But sometimes winning isn't much fun.

Lilith started to sing then, the same song—her song—clear through:

> *The goldenrod is yellow;*
> *The leaves are turning brown.*
> *The trees in apple orchard*
> *With fruit are bending down.*
>
> *The gentian's bluest fringes*
> *Are curling in the sun.*
> *In dusty pods, the milkweed*
> *Its hidden silk has spun.*

And it was much sadder than Maybelle's funeral song, but it was a sweet sadness like thinking of home when you're away.

"Gentle Grace," Lilith breathed like an amen and stood up slowly and went inside to make our tea.

THE EVENING

TOWARD THE END OF THE SUMMER, I asked if I could stay overnight with Lilith.

"We could walk out to my home place," Lilith said. "It's a lovely evening. And it's good to get your feet on the ground once in a while."

The home place. Lilith's home when she was my age. I tasted the words in my mind as we walked along the gravel road that led out of town. I knew what it would be like: a large, white house with a wide front porch, a red barn with a hay mow, and maple trees.

We walked slowly, our shadows ahead of us on the dusty road: an old woman, a young girl, and a Siamese cat.

That summer evening there was no warning of the end of day. One moment it was afternoon, the sun so hot that even the locusts stopped singing. The next moment it was dusk and for hours the land lay caught between night and day.

"The lovely twilight," Lilith said. "It's really *twice-light*, Ellen. Light from day and light from night. *Twice-light.*"

A firefly flashed at the base of a willow tree, and the frogs began to "ri-vet, ri-vet" in secret muddy places.

I heard the grating of our feet on the gravel; only Lord Jim made no sound.

"Is it much farther, Lilith? Your farm?"

She squinted down the road. "No. Just around the bend. You can see the trees from here."

Ahead Lord Jim crossed the shallow ditch into a front yard, and we followed his waving tail.

In the yard, a giant cottonwood, split by lightning, stood beside the remains of a house, lost in weeds. The roof sagged over a porch. A stalk of sunflower pushed up through a crack in the porch floor. The glass was gone from the windows. The front door hung ajar. Lord Jim, with a flick of his tail, vanished inside.

I was disappointed.

"Was there a garden?"

"There used to be. We'll look and see what's left. It's been so long."

She moved through the waist-high weeds, stopped suddenly, and pointed up into the cottonwood.

"Look up there. On that branch."

At first I saw nothing but a limb, then I saw the rusted section of a chain.

"Who could believe? Father put that up for my swing. Who'd have thought it would still be there after all this time? See? it's embedded in the wood."

I tried to imagine another girl, a Lilith, swinging and laughing when the tree was young and whole, but I couldn't.

"Let's find the garden."

"This way. Around the back. It was on the west side."

I followed Lilith, avoiding the house.

"It was here. See? There are still flowers. Day lilies. Now, come to think of it, down back by the lower well we used to have mint. I'll go down and see if there is any left. Mint grows forever, you know."

"I'll stay here."

As Lilith started down the lane, Lord Jim appeared and darted ahead of her.

My back to the house, I sat on the concrete that encircled a rusted pump and looked up at the sky. I covered my eyes and peeked out through my fingers. A hawk drifted through the clear sky. My eyes moved with the bird; I watched it sweep and glide in great circles. Suddenly it plunged out of sight.

I squeezed my eyes shut and tried to imagine another time when the house was alive. I listened for the banging of a screen door or the sounds of children playing, but except for crickets, everything was still.

The home place. I formed the words silently. I tried to imagine myself as old as Lilith and saying, like Lilith, "Yes, we left the home place when I was twelve."

My home was not like this. My house was solid and brightly painted, the spruce trees on the lawn not much taller than I. The garden was neat and free from weeds. My house would not change.

But I too would be leaving my house. At the end of the summer. I opened my eyes and watched lightning bugs glow in the drying weeds.

I had brought the news to Lilith one morning in the middle of the summer.

"We're moving the last of August."

We sat together in the kitchen while Lilith sipped her second cup of coffee.

"We're going to live in Minnapolis. There are lots of exciting things to do there. Zoos and parks. And I'm going to learn to ski."

I tried to say it as Mother had, but it didn't sound the same.

"Minneapolis, child. The vowel sounds are important. Those are the sounds that sing."

"Minneapolis," I repeated. "How far is Minneapolis?"

Lilith's eyebrows shot up under her hairline. "Well, let's find it on the map."

The atlas was scuffed and worn. On almost every page the maps had bright red circles like colorful balls.

"Why all the circles?"

"Well, some places are special and some people are special. It's good to keep track of both."

We found Minneapolis. It did not have a circle around it.

"That's not far."

"No. No farther than a whisker."

"A Lord Jim whisker?"

"But remember it took Lord Jim ten years to grow his whiskers."

AT THE HOMEPLACE, Lilith and Lord Jim walked toward me up the lane from the lower well.

"Your farm is beautiful," I said.

"Sometimes just breathing is beautiful," she answered.

It was nearly dark when we opened the gate to Lilith's house.

"How far do you think we walked?"

"Oh, a mile or two, maybe. Did it seem far?"

"No. But I was thinking, how far is ten years?"

"Ten years?" Lilith repeated. "Ten years is as far as that star . . . or as near as you." She touched my arm and guided me through the gate. "Years are for mathematicians. Not for *us*."

We rested on the back porch.

"You know. Once I thought you were terribly old."

"I am old. Even older now. A whole summer older."

"But so am I."

"Yes, you are, aren't you? And all it took to make it through our summer was to reach out across the years, didn't it? To reach out and touch across sixty-five years. Think of it. Sixty-five years. But it did take two, reaching. One from each side."

I almost told Lilith, that night on the back steps, how much I loved her, but I didn't. I think she knew.

SUMMER OVER

THE CHROME-PLATED STEEL of my ten-speed Raleigh caught the afternoon sun in a dazzle of light as I shifted the gears, leaned forward like a professional racer, and pedaled up to the cottonwood. I coasted down the hill and braked with a scrunch of tires in front of Lilith's gate. I flipped down the kick stand, and the ten-speed stood sleek and shiny—more beautiful than it ever was in Neimeyer's window.

I flung open the gate. It swung back against my ankle. Of all the days I had come and gone, I had never learned to slip through Lilith's gate quickly enough. I stooped and rubbed the spot—the same old spot. I would be scarred for life, if there were any more Lilith days left, but there weren't. The summer was over, and I had earned my bike.

On top of the clothesline post, Lord Jim dozed in the August sunlight. His eyes narrowed, but when he saw me, he dropped down, arched his back, and pushed against my legs.

Lilith stood just inside the screen door, a shadow in the glow of the late afternoon.

"Did ya see my new bike?"

"I saw it. From the window."

"Isn't it the most beautiful thing you've ever seen?"

"The most beautiful."

"Mother told me to come over and show it to you. . . . And to say good-bye."

Lilith's eyes narrowed as she held the door open.

"Flies are simply terrible." She waved her arms. "Hurry up, Lord Jim. You can move faster than that. Now, look. You silly cat. You've brought in a whole swarm."

"I can't stay very long. I'm on my way to Fran's. We're going to ride out to Wenzel's Swamp, on our bicycles."

Lilith was suddenly busy taking out the supper dishes.

"How come you're getting out two plates?"

"Mr. Cummings is coming over for dinner."

I sat down on the kitchen stool. Lord Jim jumped up into my lap.

"I don't know how . . . to say good-bye."

"Good-byes are silly anyway. Don't mean a thing."

"I guess not."

"Don't mean a thing. Summer gone. Autumn near. Winter soon." Lilith made a song of the words.

"I wish it were summer all year long. Summer all my life."

"Don't be silly. Summer is the blossoming. Autumn, the burnishing."

"And winter?"

"Winter, the rest."

"The rest of what?"

"The rest of life for which the first was made. Remember the poem?"

"Like a circle."

"Like a circle."

I stroked Lord Jim's fur.

"Did you take those books back to the library?"

"Did it last night. On the way home."

"And what about your box in the top buffet drawer?"

"I got it."

The box was an old fruit cake container Lilith had given me the day we picked up stones down along the lake shore. One was a geode, Lilith said. My five Indian Head pennies were in there too, from Mr. Cummings, and our poems . . . and the pearl ring.

"And you're moving to a new city. A new school."

"Yeah."

"It will be exciting. And different."

"I know. But I'm not afraid. And I get to ride my bike to school."

"That's nice." Lilith turned toward the sink. Lilith's back was bigger than her front.

"The summer went sort of fast, didn't it?"

"Yes. Yes, indeed it did, Ellen. For both of us."

"Funny. At first I thought it would never end."

"I know. But you see now. It's no good to look too far ahead. Best to relax and let the days wash over you."

"I learned a lot of things."

"Oh?"

"Yeah. I know what a metaphor is." Lilith had even made me learn to spell it.

"You do? That is good. Then the summer wasn't wasted?"

"We haven't even studied metaphors in school yet."

"So you'll have a head start. Now, when you learn life is a metaphor, you'll know everything."

"I'd like to know everything."

"I'll bet you would." Lilith chuckled. "So would I."

"I'll write you a letter when we get to Minneapolis."

"You do that."

I tried to think of more words, but I had run out of things to say.

"Well . . . I guess I'd better be going." I slipped from the stool and stooped to pet Lord Jim once more. "Good-bye, Lord Jim, I'm going to miss you something awful."

I looked up at Lilith's back. "Thanks for the summer."

"Good-bye, Ellen." Lilith did not turn. "And do be careful of the flies when you go out that screen door."

I slipped quickly through the door. I did not look back. The gate clanged shut behind me, and for the first time I made it through without scraping my ankle.

I wheeled the ten-speed out into the street and took one last glance over my shoulder. Lilith was standing in the porch, a silhouette in silver behind her new aluminum screens.

THE SONG ENDS

FROM MY DORMITORY WINDOW I looked down at the old snow now frozen in ugly patterns of shrunken drifts and disregarded paths. As I crumpled the newspaper clipping, the song came back—a wisp of a tune—a stray word—

Then the waver of Lilith's voice. Words, heavy for such a tiny tune. Words, bending the tune and slipping it gently into the minor:

The goldenrod is yellow,
The leaves. . . .

Words not meaning, but being.

The leaves are turning brown.
The trees in apple orchard
With fruit are bending down.

The tune recalling the words, forgotten not by intent, but by not remembering.

The gentian's bluest fringes
Are curling in the sun.
In dusty pods. . . .

The words and the tune strong now—complete. The musk of Lilith's bedroom. The ripple of her arm flesh, hanging loose, as she ran her hands through her thick hair. Ginger tea lingering sharp against my tongue.

In dusty pods, the milkweed
Its hidden silk has spun.

A Lilith, opening the world for a summer. *That* summer. The *Lilith* summer come back on a tune.

LILITH E. ADAMS, 85, PASSED
AWAY YESTERDAY AT HER HOME
AT 212 LAKE STREET.

"What does the 'E' stand for, Lilith?"
"Everlasting . . . Ellen. . . . Everlasting."

ABOUT THE AUTHORS

Hadley Irwin is the pen name of Lee Hadley and Annabelle Irwin. Both native Iowans, they teach in the English Department of Iowa State University at Ames and each has authored articles on adolescent literature. Their other juvenile novels include *We Are Mesquakie, We Are One* (The Feminist Press) and *What About Grandma?, Bring to a Boil and Separate,* and *Moon and Me* (Atheneum).

ABOUT THE FEMINIST PRESS

THE FEMINIST PRESS offers alternatives in education and in literature. Founded in 1970, this nonprofit, tax-exempt educational and publishing organization works to eliminate sexual stereotypes in books and schools and to provide literature with a broad vision of human potential. The publishing program includes reprints of important works by women, feminist biographies of women, and nonsexist children's books. Curricular materials, bibliographies, directories, and a quarterly journal provide information and support for students and teachers of women's studies. Inservice projects help to transform teaching methods and curricula. Through publications and projects, The Feminist Press contributes to the rediscovery of the history of women and the emergence of a more humane society.

Other Books for Young Readers from The Feminist Press

I'm Like Me by Siv Widerberg. Translated by Verne Moberg, drawings by Claes Backstrom. Ages 9 and up. $2.95 paper.

Tatterhood and Other Tales. Edited by Ethel Johnston Phelps, illustrated by Pamela Baldwin Ford. Ages 6 and up. $11.95 cloth, $5.95 paper.

We Are Mesquakee, We Are One by Hadley Irwin. Ages 9 and up. $7.95 cloth.

Books for Today's Young Readers: An Annotated Bibliography of Recommended Fiction for Ages 10–14. Compiled by Jeanne Bracken and Sharon Wigutoff with Ilene Baker. $4.95.

A Curriculum Guide to Women's Studies for the Middle Schools: Grades 5–9. Eileen Abrams. $4.95 paper.

Books for Children from The Feminist Press.

ABC Workbook by Jean Mangl. Drawings by Kathie Abrams. Ages 3 to 8. $2.50 paper.

A Train for Jane by Norma Klein. Illustrated by Miriam Schottland. Ages 3 to 8. $3.50 paper.

Nothing But a Dog by Bobbi Katz. Illustrated by Esther Gilman. Ages 3 to 10. $3.25 paper.

My Mother the Mail Carrier/Mi Mama la Cartera by Inez Maury. Translated by Norah E. Alemany, illustrated by Lady McCrady. Ages 4 to 9. $6.95 cloth, $3.50 paper.

Books for Today's Children: An Annotated Bibliography of Non-Stereotyped Picture Books. Compiled by Jeanne Bracken and Sharon Wigutoff. $3.95 paper.

Images of Males and Females in Elementary School Textbooks: A Slide Show. Lenore Weitzman and Diane Rizzo. Three carousels, reel or cassette tape, script and pamphlet. $300.00 plus insurance and postage.

Nonsexist Curricular Materials for Elementary Schools. Edited by Laurie Olsen. $6.95 looseleaf.